CAPTAIN SATAN:
THE DEAD MAN EXPRESS

CAPTAIN SATAN ™
KING OF DETECTIVES

THE DEAD MAN
EXPRESS

By William O'Sullivan

ALTUS PRESS • 2019

PUBLISHING HISTORY

"The Dead Man Express" originally appeared in the May 1938 (Vol. 2, No. 1) issue of *Captain Satan* magazine. Copyright © 1938 by Popular Publications, Inc. Copyright renewed © 1965 and assigned to Steeger Properties, LLC. All Rights Reserved.

CHAPTER 1
CRIME ON THE WING

C ARY ADAIR surged up out of the huge, soft-cushioned chair and strode the long length of his living room. His shoulders were hunched forward, shoulders whose real breadth was hidden by the perfect tailoring of the costly, dark-gray cloth that covered them. Strong hands, with long, tapering fingers, were clasped behind him. His polished shoes rose and fell silently in the high piling of a priceless Turkish rug.

He paused near a rare Chinese screen, gray eyes smoky, his strong mouth rebellious. The firm chin that grew out of the high, winged collar was jutted forward almost challengingly.

"Jeremy!"

A door concealed by the screen swung on silent hinges and a low, soothing voice answered "Yes, Mr. Adair?"

Cary Adair, gentleman, clubman, sportsman, Bachelor of the Art of Loafing, riveted a gray stare on his manservant. His eyes took in the man's whole, gaunt length—the sad, dark eyes set in the almost ludicrously long face—the gangling arms and abnormally long, slender, sensitive fingers—his bean-pole legs.

"What's wrong with me, Jeremy?"

The tall, slim man's eyes were sympathetic. "It's a long time since you've had any—er—*exercise*, Mr. Adair."

"Exercise!"

The wealthy bachelor's eyes glinted keenly. The corners of his

mouth softened the harsh line of the lips. He passed a browned hand thoughtfully over his sleek, dark hair. "Yes, Jeremy. That's it, that's it! Exercise!"

He snapped the starched cuff back from his left hand, revealing an expensive wristwatch strapped to a huge, powerful wrist by a platinum band. "The afternoon is half gone, thank God! Bring me a cup of black coffee with a dash of that Napoleon brandy, Jeremy."

"Yes, sir."

Adair was turning away when a sudden pounding sounded from beyond the rich hangings on the wall opposite the service pantry. Both men stiffened, stood breathlessly silent. After a moment the clatter was raised again.

"Take it," Adair said softly. He followed Jeremy across the rug with a soundless, catlike stride. In the foyer entrance beyond the living room he crossed to the trophy-hung wall, unbuttoned his coat and stood with his right hand resting lightly on his hip, his eyes narrowed.

The hammering started anew. Jeremy dropped his hand noiselessly to the polished brass knob, turned it slowly.

The door sprang open suddenly, bringing with it a gasp of surprise.

A squat, powerful, dark man in the hallway said, "Holy mackerel! Trying to scare me to death?"

Adair's face relaxed in a smile. His eyes glinted welcome. "So it's you, Jo!"

But Jeremy was coldly accusing in his gaze. "Come in, Mr. Desher." He closed the door quietly, addressed himself to Adair. "Shall I report the house telephone out of order, Mr. Adair?"

The wealthy clubman frowned suddenly, turned to Desher. But the newcomer laughed heartily as he shed his topcoat and tossed it, with the hat, to Jeremy. "That makes us even!" he boomed, his brown eyes gay. "Jeremy scared the hell out of me by jerking the door open that way. And I scared the hell out of you fellows by hammering on your door without being announced from downstairs!"

Adair's face was granite. "They have orders, downstairs," he said.

Desher grinned. "What's the use of being head of the Federal Bureau of Investigation if I can't even break into a friend's penthouse?"

"And what's the use of my owning this office building, to have this penthouse, if my orders aren't carried out?" Adair countered.

"Ha!" Desher exploded. His smile faded slightly. "I've often wondered, Cary… about this lazy life you lead. Hiding something, are you?"

Adair's eyes met with Jeremy's a brief moment, then flicked away. "Only some rare Napoleon brandy, Jo. Jeremy was just fixing me a cup of coffee with a dash of it, so I'm afraid I'm uncovered! Come in and join me in a cup." He paused while Desher transferred some venomous looking cigars from the topcoat to his jacket pocket, then led the way to the big room.

Desher's eyes were envious as they took in the quiet elegance of the place. He crossed to the full-width studio window that let out on a wide, tiled terrace, generously and tastefully studded with rare trees and plants. The F.B.I. man's gaze moved to New York Bay in the near distance. "You lucky dog! All this—and you've never even had to raise your finger for it!"

"That's what you think."

The Government investigator's eyes were covertly alert. But he didn't speak. Adair stretched out a lazy hand, index finger straight. He punched a button in the wall and the great studio door folded silently into the wall.

"I had to lift a finger that time, didn't I?" Adair laughed.

He led the way onto the terrace. Jeremy followed with the coffee and brandy.

DESHER DROPPED into a deck chair and crossed his legs. He jammed a pudgy hand into his pocket and withdrew a cigar. He bit off the tip, blew it noisily away from him. He fired the cigar, puffed up a sooty cloud of smoke.

Adair looked intently at his friend, the Government 'Sherlock Holmes' to whom Adair played a listener's part on occasion.

"Is there something up, Jo?"

Desher gulped down a swallow of the coffee and liquor and set his cup back on the saucer. He hesitated a long moment, then stared at Adair with pursed lips.

"Cary," he said, speaking slowly, "I've run right into a mystery that has me dizzy!"

Adair exhaled a long breath and settled back in his chair. He closed his eyes and rested his head comfortably. "What is it, Jo?"

The F.B.I. man puffed nervously on his cigar. "I don't know what it is about you that makes me unfold these things I run into, Cary." He pondered a moment. "I guess it's sort of… thinking out loud, for me. But I know that what I say to you never goes any further."

"I can promise you that," Adair murmured, his eyes coming wide open.

Desher stared at him. "Funny," he mused, "the way you guessed right in a couple of past cases."

"I'm a brilliant man, Jo," Adair kidded him.

"You're a lucky guesser, you mean," Desher snorted. He got to his feet and walked to the parapet that bordered the terrace, stood looking down on the busy canyon of New York's financial district. "A *very* lucky guesser!"

Adair rose, came to the man's side silently. His voice was lazily humorous when he said, "So is your mythical Captain Satan."

The F.B.I. man snapped around, his eyes hard. "What makes you say that?"

Adair looked out over the bay. "That he's mythical? Well, you've never really seen him, have you? According to your own accounts, he's always masked, or you meet him in the dark, or in the half-light." He chuckled indulgently. "Captain Satan—the private, one-man police force!"

"Go on and laugh," Desher growled. "I'm the best judge of whether or not the man is mythical. God knows, he's saved my life often enough for me to judge if he's real or not. But I didn't mean that. Why do you say he's a lucky guesser, too?"

Adair turned. "Well, he seems to be on the job whenever you lads nose into something big."

"And *how* he is! God, I'd like to get my hands on him!"

"To thank him?"

"Thank him, nothing! Oh, sure—he cracks the crooks up, turns them over to us when he's through with them—when he's gone through them like the locusts, without leaving even a coat lining to the mugs he works on!"

"So what do you care? You get the credit, don't you, Jo? Or do you tell the big-wigs in Washington that Satan did the trick for you?"

Desher shook his head sorrowfully. "The underworld knows Satan by name," he said. *"And* deed! They hate him like a plague.

And we know him, too, in the F.B.I. But—" he turned, his eyes pleading, "can you imagine what my boss would say to me if I gave him the Satan story?"

Adair grinned. "He'd probably tell you your liver was out of whack."

"At least!" Desher fell silent a moment, his eyes far away. "The man is ageless, Cary. Ageless! Twenty-five years old? Fifty years? Sixty? Take your pick. In knowledge and experience, he's a thousand years old and yet as up-to-date as a news ticker. He's stronger than an ox. He can shoot with the accuracy of a marksman, fight like a demon, run like a deer. He can ride, swim, fence like a champion. He can fly, drive a car or a speedboat like a professional—"

Adair's laugh cut in on him. "I give up, Jo! Pick up your marbles. But, what's on tap now? What brings you to New York?"

A shadow crossed Desher's face. He looked down on the silver strip that the Hudson river made in the sparkling sunlight. A barge loaded with three freight cars bugged slowly down-stream. A huge ocean liner submitted to the direction of a trio of puffing tugs as it headed for open water. A ferry boat was standing out from the Jersey shore for a downtown slip. The Federal investigator's eyes seemed to pause on... something.

"Cary," he asked, a sly smile crossing his features, "what is it that moves—that is big and bulky—that has only certain set places where it can go—and yet it can disappear and re-appear again like a will-o'-the-wisp?"

Adair pondered, his eyes following Desher's. "A steamship?"

Desher shook his head. "Boats can go to limitless places."

"Hm." Adair rubbed his chin, started suddenly "You don't mean a train?"

There was admiration in the Federal man's eyes. "By God! I think you're a mind reader!"

Adair shrugged; but his eyes were grave. "I saw you looking at something down on the river there. It had to be a boat... or those freight cars. Spill it, Jo," he said with a touch of impatience.

"Okay. Get this: A twenty-four car freight train can start from San Francisco in November, disappear in Colorado, show up in Texas in February, in Illinois in March, in Maine in April, and still deliver its cargo only two weeks late! And yet it's never been to its destination to deliver that cargo!"

"*What?*"

Desher nodded soberly. "Now get ready for another shock, Cary. That very train, the very cars on that string, were seen in three different places, thousands of miles apart... *at the very same hours on identical days!*"

"Phantom cargoes!" Adair whispered, his eyes blazing with excitement.

CHAPTER 2
DEATH ON WHEELS

DESHER WALKED to the small table and drained the rest of his coffee. " 'Phantom cargoes' is a swell description of it, Cary," he said, wiping his mouth with the back of his hand. "But the queer part of it is, no one is complaining."

Adair's face was a study. "Jo," he said slowly, "do you talk, or do I wring the story out of you?"

"I talk. The railroads are shut tighter than clams about the matter. The people to whom the freight is consigned—every last one of them—are politely dumb when we question them. Yet the instance I just quoted—the train that was all over the United States at one and the same time—is only one of a dozen."

"Then how did you find out about it?"

"One small manufacturer squawked, Cary. Called us on the telephone from New York and said he had a queer tale to tell us… about freight shipments."

"And?" Adair prompted.

"We told him to come along to our New York offices—told him not to waste a minute. He didn't waste even a second, it seems. He hurried. He came in such a hurry that he fell down his own elevator shaft, in his rush, and was killed."

"Good Lord!"

Desher nodded slowly. "Odd, eh? Well, we put our undercover men to work when the railroads and the other shippers involved wouldn't talk."

"With what results?"

"I'm telling you, Cary. In fact, I've told you. The thing ends there. We're up against a blank wall. Further, we're working on a limited budget in the F.B.I. We can't very well spend all our money in investigating things that apparently don't exist."

"But they *do* exist," Adair snapped, his voice tense. "You've said so yourself."

Desher puffed at his cigar, found it dead. He hurled it over the parapet and reached for another and lit it.

"It's a bit of a mystery," he said. "But aside from that, other than mere curiosity on our part, we have no reason to follow it further."

"Then why are you in New York?"

"Routine. Just one final check-up. The last train to disappear had a shipment of fiber that's peculiar to one of the Philippine Islands. It is so rare as to be a monopoly, controlled by the manufacturer to whom it was consigned."

"But what makes you think he'll talk?"

"Nothing. I merely hope he will. If he doesn't, then I'm through. But, Cary—we had a check on this train, as we have had on all others, when it left 'Frisco. The train never got to Chicago. It was checked back through Salt Lake City this morning. Yet the cargo was delivered to the manufacturer yesterday!"

Adair was frowning his wonder when the F.B.I. official burst his bombshell.

"And that train," he said slowly, "that string of cars that was in Salt Lake City this morning, is in the freight terminal in this city—*in this city*—while I'm sitting here talking to you."

"Impossible!" Adair almost shouted. "It's too fantastic, Jo."

Desher pulled a paper from his inside jacket-pocket. On it were typed a row of numerals and initials. "This," he said, wagging the thing under Adair's nose, "is the list of numbers telegraphed to us from Salt Lake City by our operative. It happens to be the numbers of that train—car for car, and the Lines which own them—that left 'Frisco with that fiber shipment. *It is also the list of the cars that are in the New York freight terminal this very minute!*"

Adair had settled back into his chair again, his features frozen in attention. "What are your plans? What do you do now?"

Before Desher spoke, Adair looked meaningly at Jeremy, standing in the doorway.

"I talk with the manufacturer," Desher said with a trace of bitterness. "As usual, he doesn't know what it's all about. Then I go to the yards and check the freight car numbers."

"And then?"

"Then, I file a confidential report in Washington and forget about the whole thing." He added with a laugh, "That's how we spend our time and money."

Adair nodded. "But the file is there if any trouble ever pops from this thing. You're that much further than if you started from scratch, should a squawk ever come." He hesitated a moment. Then: "Are you going to these places alone?"

"Sure. Nothing to it. Why?"

"I'd like to go with you," Adair said. Desher shrugged. "That's simple. I can introduce you as one of my operatives." He guffawed suddenly and slapped a hand on his thigh. "Man, that's a good one! Cary Adair, the gentleman loafer, working as a secret operative!" He was convulsed with laughter for a moment. But when he saw his friend's eyes harden, he said, "I'm sorry, Cary. But you don't know how funny that is."

Adair got to his feet and stretched. "Maybe I do!"

THE HASSEM Products Company was housed in a dingy warehouse-and-factory in the lower East Side of New York. After waiting five minutes for the elevator, Desher started for the wooden stairs. A sign read, *Office Two Flights Up.*

"Come on. Let's get this over with."

Adair followed. The stairs doubled back at the first landing, and the F.B.I. man turned, started up the second flight. Adair paused, his eyes on a steel door that bore the admonition *'Keep Out.'* He stepped over, pulled the door open, and looked in.

Some men in overalls were sorting out bulky, square bales, dragging them along the worn floors of the place to pile them in rows at the far end of the long room. One of the workers looked up.

"Can'tcha read?" he barked at Adair. "Shut that door! G'wan, get outa here!"

Adair stepped into the room, came slowly across the floor. "Isn't this the office?" he asked mildly. "Isn't this the second flight up?"

The other, obviously the foreman of the crew, looked over his shoulder; furtively, Adair thought. He came forward quickly. "Listen, mister, the office is on the floor above. I told you to—"

"What's the trouble?"

Adair swung, at that new voice that came from behind him. A short, hard-eyed, swarthy man stood there, his hands thrust into his jacket pockets. Adair stiffened when he saw the ominous bulge of the concealed right hand. But his smile was disarming.

"No trouble. I'm just looking for the office."

There was a sudden hammering on the door. Before anyone could speak or move, even, the door crashed open and Jo Desher strode in. The wiry man who stood in front of Desher took his hands from his pockets suddenly. Adair heard him mutter "It's okay" to the foreman, before he turned and went quietly back into a small cubicle in the front of the room.

"I got mixed up," Adair smiled at the F.B.I. man. "I thought you came in here."

They went out and up the stairs, Desher shaking his head sorrowfully at such stupidity. A girl at a switchboard stopped chewing gum long enough to ask what they wanted. The F.B.I. man flashed his badge quickly, but didn't give the girl time to see exactly what it was.

"I'm here to see the boss," he snapped. "I'm from the freight yards."

"Oh!" The girl plugged in a wire and said, "There's a railroad dick here to see you, Mr. Hassem. Send him in? Okay." She pulled the plug out, thumbed at a door. "Okay, Sherlock."

Adair grinned at the sight of Desher's reddened face. And he winked at the operator when she let her eyes slide over his expensive outfit and bridled coyly at him.

"He's my stooge," Adair said easily.

"Who wouldn't be?" the girl cracked back, her eyes openly flattering.

The door led into a narrow hall. At the end of it stood two

men. "This way, please," one of them called, a fat, dark-skinned man. His companion stood close to him but silent, watchful.

Desher nodded curtly. "Your name Hassem?" he addressed the larger of the two. "You get your cargo all right?"

Adair saw beads of perspiration spring alive on the man's forehead. Nor did his eyes miss the convulsive twitch of the Adam's apple. "Wha—what cargo?"

"Let's not beat around the bush," Desher snapped.

The man at Hassem's side laughed suddenly, a queer, dead-voiced laugh. Adair swung and looked at him squarely for the first time. He blinked at the peculiar pallor of Hassem's companion—a yellowish, parchment-like skin that accented a large, hairy mole on the left cheek.

But the most arresting features were the man's eyes—large, but without any life, any sparkle, and abnormally protruding. His hair was heavy and jet black, ending in a too perfect line at his collar.

"He's bald," Adair reasoned, "and vain. Else why would he wear a toupée, a wig?" He watched alertly as the man faced Desher.

"No, let's not beat around the bush," the odd-looking individual said, after his jarring laugh. "You're a railroad detective? Where are your credentials?"

Desher blinked. "Who's he?"

Hassem shrugged; but he was plainly nervous. "A—partner."

The one designated as a 'partner' turned his dead stare onto Adair. "And who is *he?*" he asked, his voice contemptuously amused.

15

Desher turned, pinned the man with a bleak eye. "He's a partner of mine."

"Good!" The strange-looking one showed large, dead-white teeth in a smile. "We're all partners. Cozy, isn't it?" His mouth closed with a snap and he lidded his eyes momentarily. "Where are your credentials?"

Desher tried to ignore him, addressed himself directly to Hassem. "You had a cargo consigned by freight from San Francisco that was delivered last night. Everything all right? It wasn't delayed too long in transit?" But it was no go.

"Where are your credentials? Who sent you? What railroad do you represent? Who said anything about a cargo? What do you want here?" The other man asked.

Desher turned on his tormentor in a fury. "Will you shut up?"

"No. I won't. But you will!"

Hassem wiped his moist face with a handkerchief. "No use to get excited," he said nervously. He edged slightly away from Desher's tormentor. "There wasn't no cargo. We don't know what you're talking about."

The smaller man moved with him, though, standing slightly behind. "You shut up, too!" He seemed to nudge his 'partner.' Hassem trembled and closed his shaking lips.

Adair's eyes narrowed slightly and he horned in. "What's *your* name?" he asked the pop-eyed individual.

Those lifeless eyes focused on him a long moment, then lidded again suddenly. "John Smith," came the sneering reply.

Desher shrugged his shoulders, quelled the rage that was

apparent in his face. "Well, we must have got things wrong down at the railroad," he said lamely. "Guess we'll be going."

Neither Hassem nor his companion spoke as the two went down the hall to the exit.

"YOU SEE?" Desher said, opening his hands expressively. "Not a word of information. Yet we know that there is something wrong—someplace."

Adair stared out the window of their speeding taxi. "What did you make of our friend Mr. John Smith?"

"Just a crabbed little runt," Desher dismissed him.

Adair shook his head. "I certainly wouldn't let anyone talk to me that way if I were Chief of the F.B.I."

"He's within his rights," Desher said. "The Government can't horn into a man's affairs unless there is something definitely wrong, or if it is invited." He grinned ruefully. "He sure sized me up in a rush!"

Adair was thoughtful. The cab crossed over Fourteenth Street, then bent uptown on the West Side. "That little fellow in the storeroom seemed to size you up, too."

"Huh? Which was that?"

"The wiry, tough looking man I was talking to when you came in. Remember?"

"I didn't notice especially," Desher said. "What did he do?"

"He wheeled right away from there when you came through the door."

"He did?" The taxi slid to a stop and the driver looked back through the window. "Here we are," Desher said, and yanked the door open.

They crossed the avenue and headed for the open freight yards. A watchman let them pass when Desher flashed his badge. The F.B.I. man went swiftly down a long line of stationary freight cars, crossed several parallel tracks, made his way along another line of closed cars. A low whistle stopped him.

Desher whipped around, looked up into the air. Adair's eyes followed. An oil-stained man in overalls was standing atop a car, staring down at them. "Hi, Chief," he said. "This is the string." His eyes flicked Adair.

Desher nodded. "Anything odd about it? You talked with the train crew?"

"Talked with 'em all." The man considered a moment. "There's something screwy going on, chief, but for the life of me I can't make it out."

"The cars all okay? You took samples of dust from the floors?"

"I did. It's the same fiber that the Hassem outfit uses. But they got the stuff delivered yesterday, and this string came in only this morning."

Desher shook his head angrily. "Well, forget it, Peyton. We've got enough for our files. Give me the list of names of the train crews, from 'Frisco on in, and get back to your regular assignment."

"Okay." The man fetched a paper from his pocket and tossed it to Desher.

They started across the tracks again. Desher dropped all thought of the thing, apparently, until Adair spoke.

"No ideas on it at all, Jo?"

"Might be some sort of railroad war starting," Desher

hazarded. "Or a shippers' union cracking down on certain groups. But I dunno. What are your plans, Cary?"

Adair averted his eyes. "Oh, maybe I'll take a little cruise somewhere," he said. "I'm bored with New York. Nothing much doing around here."

The F.B.I. man snorted. "You lucky scoundrel! Just nothing to do but bum around. Where to this time?"

"Oh—Mexico, maybe. Or out into the old Indian country of the West." He paused to let a yard engine's loud puffing and shrill whistle die down. "But I don't know exactly where, or how long I'll be—"

Desher slammed him in the chest savagely, knocking him back from a track he was crossing. *"Look out!"* the F.B.I. man screamed madly.

Adair leaped mightily and sprawled out of danger. A hot breath of steam licked over him as a locomotive roared by on the track, inches away.

Adair picked himself up slowly and stared after the engine.

"The damn' fool might have hit us!" Joe Desher growled. "He ought to be more careful."

"He certainly should," Adair said with a little laugh. "I'm afraid that man is headed for trouble."

Into his mind came the picture of that man at the factory... of the man 'John Smith,' whom Hassem had introduced as his partner. He was seeing again those oddly lifeless, large eyes, that yellowed skin... seeing that hideous face again as he had seen it at Hassem's side—

And again as it had looked down at him from the cab of that speeding locomotive, as Adair lay sprawled on his back.

CHAPTER 3
A FLASH IN THE DARK

DESHER STOPPED briefly at Adair's downtown office building on his way to Newark Airport. He shook his head when he entered the private express elevator that ran to the penthouse.

"I imagine you're the only man in New York who lives atop a busy office building," he said.

"I'm not," Adair contradicted. "But I may be the only one who is this far downtown. This is the only spot where I could get everything I wanted. Absolute quiet at night, *and* privacy... a view of the bay and the busy river traffic...." He paused. "Besides, Jo, it's only seconds from here to the Holland Tunnel into Jersey, or across the lower bridge to Long Island."

Desher grunted. "As though you were ever in a hurry to go anywhere!"

The door of the apartment swung open as they quit the elevator. Jeremy stood, woodenly impassive, to let them enter.

"Now, how did you know we were coming up?" the F.B.I. man asked, his eyes round.

Adair smiled slightly. "I have a secret signal to announce myself." He passed Jeremy his hat, topcoat and walking-stick. "Have a highball, Jo? Good! Make it two, Jeremy." He raised his voice slightly as he went into the living room.

"That list of names your operative dropped you from the freight train?" he asked, his voice casual. "You have it? In your coat?"

"I should say not! Papers like that go in my wallet!"

When Jeremy served the highballs, he found a speck of ash to dust from Desher's jacket lapel. "Those cigars," he murmured reprovingly. The F.B.I. man watched him disappear into the pantry and chuckled.

"Some lad, that Jeremy! Has he ever smiled or laughed that you know of?"

Adair pursed his lips, appeared to consider the matter gravely. "I know he's often had reason to," he said judiciously. "Well, here's luck, Jo. And may the phantom cargoes meet a superior ghost!"

Desher frowned slightly; but he drained his drink in three gulps and stood to his feet. "Nice seeing you, Cary. I've got to—"

Adair sprang to his feet, "Oh, but you *can't* go now, Jo. Not yet. Have another drink, Jo!"

Desher shrugged briefly, then dropped into his chair again. "Well, just one."

Jeremy appeared as if by magic, a silver tray in his hand, two tall, tinkling, amber-fluid glasses on the tray. "Here you are, sir."

Desher set his drink down to light a cigar. Jeremy slid the tray on the table and snapped a match alive. But he dropped it as Desher puffed… dropped it on the investigator's lapel. With a smothered exclamation of horror, Adair's servant slapped the ember to the floor.

"Sorry, sir." He faced Adair. "Shall I get Mr. Desher's things ready for him now, Mr. Adair?"

Desher took a long pull at his drink and stood up again.

Adair said, "All right, Jeremy." He coughed once. "Yes; Mr. Desher has to rush away."

At the door, he shook hands warmly. "It was decent of you to let me tag along to-day, Jo."

The Government man laughed. "I hope the excitement wasn't too much for you, Cary. Have a nice trip!"

"I'll do my best," Adair said as Desher entered the elevator. He shut the door and turned to Jeremy. The servant was staring inquiringly.

"Jeremy, old chap, I think that a trip is in order!"

"Yes, sir?"

Adair considered, his eyes narrowed. "You—ah—can pack quickly?"

"I'm always ready, sir."

"Of course. You have a packing list to go by?"

The corners of Jeremy's mouth turned upward slightly. "I have all manner of lists, sir."

Adair smothered a grin. "Right, Jeremy. Well, I'll shave and change. We'll be out of here by dark!"

A FILM of clouds obscured the moon. A sleek, black car slipped noiselessly down a deserted street on the lower East Side. It slowed as it came opposite a deserted factory building, then slid ahead and around the corner.

Several minutes later, two shadowy figures clung close to the building line and came back down the street. They paused at a door marked *THE HASSEM PRODUCTS COMPANY.* The taller of the two wraiths produced a ring of keys, started fitting one after another of them into the lock. The second man—shorter, broader, more muscular—turned his back and watched up and down the street.

He turned at a sudden *click*, vanished through the now opened door. It shut again on a deserted street.

There was the merest whisper of feet as they went up the wooden stairs of the place to the first landing, then mounted slowly to the floor above. There was another pause, another fitting of a skeleton key, then the office door clicked shut.

Without any more light than was cast by a street lamp reflected from the ceiling of the offices, the two figures went straight to another door, down a darkened passage.

"This is it—right ahead of us," a sibilant whisper announced. "Sixteen paces, exactly. I counted them."

"Right, Captain!"

The door swung silently. The tall, gaunt figure crossed quickly to the window and the shade was lowered, plunging the room into absolute blackness. A strong beam from a flashlight sprang alive and swung unerringly to a large black safe in one corner.

"Work fast, Slim! Remember, the boys are waiting at the new headquarters."

"Right, Captain."

The longer shadow materialized into a tall, gangling-armed man whose masked features were set off by the blue-white ray. He stooped, set his ear close to the combination dial, and twirled the disc rapidly, first left, then right. Three minutes later he straightened and pressed down on the safe handle.

The stout black door opened soundlessly. But the two men stiffened. Somewhere in the stillness a muffled noise echoed. The ray of light died, and with it all life seemed to go from the room.

"Rats, probably," a whisper came after a long five minutes. The flash jumped into being again, focused on the interior of the safe. The second of the two men crossed to it quickly, lifted out two ledgers with his strong, browned hands. He set them on the desk of the place, flipped one of the books open. The flashlight brought the entries on the pages into dear relief... stopped suddenly.

"Here's the first of this year, Slim. Open up that other book."

The light searched through the pages as they were turned one after another. Then: "Hold it!" A low chuckle broke the sudden silence. "Just what I thought! Hassem keeps double books. Okay, Slim. Turn those pages slowly, while I turn these."

"Right, Captain."

The pages of both books were swung methodically, and the muscular figure, who had been addressed as "Captain," finally said, "This is just what I expected! Hassem has these books fixed up beautifully. Come on, Slim, I've seen all I want to see!" But both men froze into immobility.

A third voice had joined the group. "And all you're going to see!" that new voice said ominously.

The flashlight snapped off, but another light took its place... an orange-red streak that jutted suddenly and with a deafening roar from the door that had opened so silently. Three times, that gun crashed in the still of the small office.

Then a new light sprang into being, the glow of a weirdly blue lamp growing from the floor behind the desk and blazing brightly on the ceiling.

And in the center of that new light crouched a silhouetted figure of a horned devil with pitchfork upraised menacingly.

A choking gasp came from the door.

"Satan! Captain Satan!"

The full-throated bellow of a heavy automatic roared twice, drowning that terrified gasp, stilling that voice for all time. There was a heavy crash as the man fell to the floor.

Instantly, the lamp shifted from the ceiling, searched out the still form that lay stretched out in the doorway. "Come on, Slim! We've got to break clear!"

"Right, Captain."

But the lamp stopped as its ray crossed the features of the dead man.

"Good Lord, Captain, you drilled him twice through the same hole in the forehead!"

The lamp dipped suddenly. A browned hand holding a fountain pen came into its light, quickly sketched a figure on the back of the dead man's hand… on the hand of the small, wiry, swarthy-faced gunman.

"He must have—" the pen sketched on rapidly, surely—"had a trick alarm rigged up to the safe. That thud we heard, instead of a bell. A neat trap!" The pen stopped, added another line. "He was the downstairs guard."

The light grew large again. On the dead man's hand was sketched a replica of the figure that had sprung alive so frighteningly on the ceiling but a moment before. A harsh chuckle sounded in the room.

"It's only polite to leave your calling card!"

A police car siren raised a banshee wail in the distance as the place was plunged once again into darkness.

Captain Satan's pitchfork was in the ring!

CHAPTER 4
SATAN'S CREW

IT WAS an eerie crew that was gathered in the deserted warehouse. Eight masked men stood in a line against the wall, their figures lighted by the Satan lamp. Candles flickered on a packing case far in the rear. The high windows of the place were blocked out with shields of heavy matting.

Squarely in the center of the room stood a broad-shouldered, masked man whose close-fitting, somberly black clothes revealed a powerfully muscled body. The lights danced on the man's bleak gray eyes as he riveted them on the eight still figures. His hair was cropped close, and the black silk shirt and tie of the man made his tanned face accentuatedly darker.

Behind him and slightly to one side stood a gaunt, long-legged man whose mask split a morose face. In his slender, sensitive fingers he held a sheaf of papers.

The powerfully built man snapped, "Call the roll, Slim!"

"Right, Captain." The gaunt one's eyes peered through the

black slits at the first of the various papers he held. "Gentleman Dan?"

"Here, Slim." A tall, graceful, debonair man with waxed mustache and patent-leather hair stepped lazily forward. His black eyes glinted in the candlelight beyond the two central figures.

"Fingerprints," the leader snapped.

Slim stepped forward. "I think, Captain, that if we identify Doc first and let him take the prints, that it would go faster."

"All right. Doc?"

A gray-haired man, slightly stooped and small in stature, stepped forward. "Here, Cap'n." He advanced and took the needle and the small bottle of alcohol which Slim tendered him. Carefully, he jabbed the sharp thing into a finger, squeezed out some blood. He put the red tip carefully on the paper that Slim held firm for him.

Satan's lieutenant looked at the print it made, compared it with another that was on the same paper. "Doc passes."

Satan turned, a smile easing his severe features. He thrust out a hand. "Glad to see you, Doc."

"Glad to be with you again, Cap'n," the little man answered. He stepped over to where Gentleman Dan stood, quickly printed him.

"Gentleman Dan passes," Slim intoned solemnly.

"Glad to see you, Dan," Satan said.

One after another, Satan's crew came as they were called. Pat—short and husky, blue eyes twinkling in a ruddy face that was set off by a wispy, carrot-colored mustache. Pat scratched his sparse red hair as he greeted his leader with the faintest touch of a brogue.

Soapy—a moth-eaten, furtive, bald and weazened individual with pale eyes.

Kayo—powerfully built, with the meaty shoulders of a wrestler, his black, curly hair glistening with oil. A flatly broken nose spread wide under the mask he wore.

Solly—a long-beaked, thin little man whose eyes were alert as two small animals. Satan eyed him with a grin. And The Dutchman—fat, blond, blue-eyed and jolly.

One after another, as they were fingerprinted for identification, Satan greeted his men. He was cordial, but there was in his manner that which called for speed. His men complied.

Satan turned to Slim. "The new man?"

Slim crossed to a door over against one wall, opened it. He came back leading a rangy man whose eyes were tightly blindfolded and from whose ears wisps of soft cotton hung.

"Places, men," Satan snapped. "Slim! Take off the blindfold, mask him, pull the cotton out of his ears." He turned. "Who speaks for this man?"

Gentleman Dan nodded. "I do, Cap'n."

SATAN LOOKED squarely into the eye slits of the newcomer's mask. Then he stepped back, sized the man up carefully, impressed on his mind every smallest detail of his build.

"What is your purpose here, stranger?" he asked harshly.

"*To become a blood brother,*" the man answered soberly, in the ritual which his spokesman had rehearsed with him.

"Why?"

"To join with the others of Satan's Crew in fighting Satan's appointed enemies; to obey orders implicitly; to maintain the secrecy of our organization and to seek not the identities of the other members, nor to reveal my own, save to Satan and his lieutenant. And to defend unto death myself and my brothers."

Satan nodded. "Gentleman Dan has hinted at what our group is. Let me tell you, briefly, what our *purpose* is. First—we are not a band organized to oppose the Law of the land. Understand that! Our enemies are the Law's enemies. But sometimes we have to—er—*circumvent* the organized police to reach our goal."

There was a guffaw from the veteran line. Satan pinned a bleak eye on Pat. "Our former flatfoot member seems to think it's funny," he observed mildly. "But it isn't half as funny as one time *he* tried to stop us—and ended up tied to the torch of the Statue of Liberty!"

There was a general laugh and Pat subsided ruefully. Satan grinned. "Never mind, Pat. A sense of humor is better than a grouch any day." He continued:

"We are, in effect, a private police force that collects its pay from the crooks. And it's good pay!"

"You're telling us!" Solly gurgled. But he shut up at Satan's look.

"Whatever the booty is, I take one-third and the rest is split in even shares among you men. Of course, I pay all expenses while you men are working with me. That's the system."

"And what a seestem!" Solly crowed. "You won't be sorry, mister."

"Slim! A thousand dollars fine against Solly."

"Oi, oi!"

"*Two* thousand dollars fine!"

"*Oi*, oi, *oi, oi*, oi!"

Gentleman Dan choked. Slim turned his head away. The next moment the grim warehouse was echoing to roars of laughter from as menacing looking a crew as ever assembled under one roof. Satan himself broke after a moment. When he sobered, he said:

"Remit the fine, Slim. But only if Solly stays shut! We have serious business to attend to."

"Right, Captain."

"Now, stranger—how stand you?"

"As one of Satan's Crew," the big, silent man answered steadily.

"You will be fingerprinted in blood," Satan said slowly, "because it is a symbol. You will be called upon to shed blood, if necessary, to smash the crooks and racketeers who are our enemies. Sometimes," he added sadly, "it might mean your own blood... your life's blood!"

There was a grim silence as the men recalled the companions of other campaigns who had died in the fight.

"I still so desire," the man made answer.

"Fingerprint him, give him his call-letter instructions when you've adopted a name," Satan ordered Slim.

When the big fellow's prints had been taken, he said simply, "They call me Hank." He moved embarrassedly, ducked his head. "My—my real name is... Percival."

Slim grinned. "I think we'll stick to Hank as a name. Now, get this—*and never forget it!* We have a secret system of conveying

They leaped from in front
of the locomotive.

our names to one another, In case of extreme emergency and need. It is this—you use the *first* and the *last* letters of your crew name. Understand?"

Hank nodded soberly. "My call letters are 'Aitch-kay?'"

"You've got it, Hank."

Satan stepped close and shook the man's hand. "Glad to have

you with us, Hank. What is your specialty… in—er—civilian life?"

"I'm a retired railroad man."

Satan's eyes met Slim's and a wide grin grew on the leader's face. "A good omen," he murmured. "Luck is starting on our side!"

Slim finished his instructions. "You have a telephone, of course. When you're not on assignment, you'll stay on or near that 'phone *night and day!* That clear?"

"That's clear," Hank answered evenly.

"Attention to orders," Satan barked.

The new man lined up with the veterans. Slim snapped a pad and pencil out of a pocket, noted the orders in shorthand as Satan spoke rapidly, incisively.

"**THERE IS** a new twist being applied to an old racket," the leader said, his eyes cold, his voice hard. "Obviously, it's a shakedown on freight shipments, but with this difference:

"The gang that is operating it has injected a mystery element—and has succeeded in throttling both the receivers *and* the rail lines. The Government has investigated… and withdrawn again. They can't get to first base with it. Naturally, the railroads have their own detectives working on it, too."

Satan paused to light a cigarette. He used a round, enamel-and-gold automatic lighter, slid it back into his pocket.

"The shakedown is plenty! Slim and I verified that to-night—and left a dead gangster branded with the Satan mark to let the crooks know we're in the ring! I'm not going to go into what I already know of this thing. We'll start from scratch and track this thing down from the letter 'A' to the letter 'Z'—and the letter 'Z' will be the crooks' finish… *or ours!*"

The men stirred restlessly, Satan's forceful manner having its effect on them. They were like hunting dogs straining on the leash.

"You, Doc! Get around to the morgue and to the undertaking parlors and see what you can find about a man who was shot through the forehead. Shot twice through the same spot! Trace the dead man's connections if you can find the body."

"Right, Cap'n."

"Soapy! Get around in the underworld and dig up some information on a man—" Satan paused slightly—"a man with large, dark pop-eyes and a hairy mole on his left cheek. He's bald, but probably wears a wig."

"Huh?" Then, at Satan's glare: "Excuse me, Cap'n. But… it sounded so much like Jake Largo—"

"He's dead," Satan snapped. "Killed twenty years ago, a bullet through his brain."

Soapy blinked. "Right, Cap'n. I *seen* him dead!"

"Solly! You're an out-of-town buyer, interested in the products of the Hassem Company. Slim will fix you with the proper papers, from some out-of-town concern…."

"Oi, Cap'n," Solly marveled. "You own beesnesses, too!"

"Quiet! Pat—Gentleman Dan—The Dutchman—you're railroad men, out of work. And you don't want any, either! But Slim will give you cards of identification and you can go to the yards and talk of your tough luck in not landing jobs. Keep your ears open… *and your eyes!* This is a tough, smart gang we are up against."

Gentleman Dan shook his head and stared at his carefully manicured hands. *"Me* a railroad worker, with these hands, Cap'n?"

"Conductor or dispatch man. Telegraph operator. Make it anything you want. You might drop a hint that you're one tough baby with a gun." Satan smiled slightly. "God knows you can back *that* up!"

"Right, Cap'n."

Satan swung to the new man. "Hank!"

"Yes, Captain?"

Satan shook his head. "There's only one man in the crew that calls me 'Captain.' That's Slim. To the rest of you, I am 'Cap'n.'"

"Right, Cap'n."

"Hank, I want you to trace—" Satan reached out a hand and Slim passed him a paper, "freight train number 111, out of San Francisco on April the fifteenth. And when I say trace, *I mean trace!* Check the *stations* it was reported through—the *time* it was reported through, the *next* station at which it showed—the mileage *between* them." He paused, turned to Slim.

"Give Hank plenty of expense money, Slim. Say… twenty-five hundred to start."

"Cap'n?" The new man's head was cocked to one side. "That's going to take time."

"Three days," Satan snapped. "You'll take a plane to-night. Charter one, if you must." He looked at a paper again. "Know anything about the S.D. & R. Line?"

34

Hank grinned. "Worked on it ten years, Cap'n."

"Will that speed it up any?"

"Can I 'phone my report, Cap'n?"

"If it's important enough, yes."

"Make it *two* days, Cap'n."

"Good. Slim will distribute guns, ammunition, money, identification papers." The leader turned back to the railroad man. "Is it usual for the same freight crew to take a train right through from the West Coast to New York?"

"No, Cap'n." The railroad man frowned. "Never."

"That's what happened in this case," Satan said impatiently. "So don't say 'never.'"

The new man shrugged and lapsed silent. Satan signaled to Kayo. "You'll drive me," he said simply.

"Right, Cap'n." A huge grin further flattened the big fellow's nose under the black silk mask. He rubbed his big hands together gleefully. Kayo was a driving hellion and loved nothing better than a speedy car under the seat of his pants.

Satan came close to Slim. "Get your work through as quickly as you can, Slim. We've got a little interviewing to do."

His lieutenant's eyebrows went up in surprise, moving the mask comically. Satan said softly:

"I'd like to know why these freight train lads came all the way from 'Frisco to New York!"

35

CHAPTER 5
BULLETS SPEAK LAST

KAYO PARKED the powerful car in an alleyway and went quickly to the building line, to stand watch. Satan and Slim climbed a rickety fence and tried one of the grimy rear windows of the cheap hotel on the riverfront. When it didn't give, Slim slid a jimmy into place and applied gentle pressure. Before they climbed in, Satan spotted the trunk-and-junk laden room with his flash… climbed after it.

"Storeroom," he said.

Slim followed him in. A door at the far end gave onto a small hall that led to the stairs. Cautiously they crept up, pushed open the door at the first landing.

A clerk slept behind the desk, his snores waking the echoes in the dingy lobby. Satan slid around the door and Slim followed quickly. The two adjusted their guns as they went… slipped them into armpit holsters.

On the third floor, Satan looked at a door number. "It's down here to the left," he whispered. Further down, they stopped. Satan tried a door, gently. It was locked. The flash showed the key in the door, on the inside.

Slim unfolded a square of smooth paper, slipped it under the door. With slender tweezers, he turned the key from the outside until it was straight up and down in the lock. Then he pushed. A clunk told him the key had dropped. He drew out the paper carefully and passed the key to Satan. In a moment they were inside.

A stir sounded against one of the walls. Then, "Who is that?"

Satan's flashlight jumped alive, beat into the sleepy eyes of a tousled-haired man. "You won't be harmed if you keep still," he said.

The man in bed blinked in the light, then laughed sleepily. "You're in the wrong place to rob a man, pardner!"

Satan said, "You won't be robbed."

The occupant of the room stared into the light that speared at him. He was nervous, but plainly unafraid. "What the hell do you want?" he growled.

"To ask you a few questions," Satan said, his voice going hard. "And you'd better answer them straight or you'll be very, very sorry."

The man yawned and started to sit up. Satan's gun jumped into his hand. "Just lie back there and take it easy. Why did you come east on Train One-eleven?"

The railroad man's eyes stared steadily into the light. "I— don't know."

"You have orders not to talk?"

"You know the answers, pardner!"

"But you will talk!"

The man grinned slightly. "Oh, no I won't."

Satan snapped, "Okay, Slim!" The lieutenant stepped forward, jammed his automatic close to the man's head. The railroad hand started suddenly, then lay back with a sigh of resignation.

"All right, all right! But you won't get any more out of it than I know. And *I* don't know anything!"

"*What?*"

"I was on the crew that left with One-eleven on April 15th from San Francisco. Some time before we reached Tonopah—that's Nevada—I lay down in the caboose to take a sleep." The man paused, his eyes going puzzled.

"Come on! What's the rest of it?"

"I woke up in Jersey City two days ago," he answered simply.

Satan's flash came closer, focused on the man's neck, his hair, his arms. "You're a liar!"

"If you think I am, shoot!"

Satan stood silent a moment. Then: "What's your normal weight?"

"One seventy-nine or so."

"That's about what you weigh now."

"Right."

"So, if you've been asleep all this time, without food, without water, without exercise, what has you alive now—*at your normal weight?*"

The man shrugged. "You tell me. And I'll tell the road dicks."

"They've questioned you on every angle of it?" Satan asked the chap.

The man nodded. "Not only questioned us. They're watching us like a cat looking down a rat hole. Every second!"

Slim made a sound. "Watching you—*now?*"

"Sure. I don't leave the hotel without one of them tailing me. And they won't let me talk with the other men on the crew. It's sure got me on the ropes, mister!"

Satan started suddenly. There were sounds coming from beyond the door... footsteps. The leader snapped his light off.

But the sounds came nearer. A heavy tread halted outside the door and there was a sharp rap.

"What's going on in there? I seen a light from the street!"

The three were silent in the dark, Slim jamming his gun against the railroad man's throat. But the pounding started again. "Come on! Open up, you!"

With a sigh, Satan snapped the flash on again and motioned with it to Slim. "I'll start him. You frisk him… while he's on his way, if you can!"

SATAN MADE the few steps to the door with catlike steps, called "Wait a minute" in a muffled, sleepy voice. He rattled the key in the lock—but didn't turn it. Then:

"Push, will you?" he called to the man on the other side. "The door seems to be stuck!"

There was a moment's pause, then the thud of a body against the door, a grunt when the portal didn't open. Satan turned the key noiselessly, eased the knob in a half twist. The man outside tried again. The door crashed open and the outsider stumbled heavily across the floor, lost his balance, fell.

Slim was on him in a flash, pouncing like a wrestler. The man on the floor cursed, collapsed with a groan as a dull *thwack* sounded in the darkness. Satan swiftly transferred the key to the outside of the door. Slim stood a moment looking at the man in the bed, the light from the hall casting a menacing glow across those two masked faces in the door.

Then he drifted into the hallway. Satan pulled the door shut, turned the key. They had reached the head of the stairs when the rumpus started in that room they had quit.

"I got his gun and badge," Slim panted, as they rounded the lobby turn and made for the basement. Both men stopped dead when the sound of firing crashed in the stillness of the night, outside.

"Kayo!" Satan barked. "Hurry, Slim."

They swarmed out the storeroom window, hurled themselves over the fence. Three more shots awakened the echoes of the empty streets. As they came into view of the car, they saw a shadow crouched by the alley wall. A flash of orange flame came from beyond the parked car's hood. The shadow threw two in answer.

Satan whipped his automatic from his arm holster and took careful aim. He pulled the trigger. A scream of pain came from the crouching figure. Slim stepped near, trained his flashlight on a man who writhed in pain on the ground and clutched a gory right hand. With a deft snap he brought his clubbed automatic down. The man stilled.

Kayo came out from beyond the hood of the car and ghosted into his seat. Satan and Slim clambered into the rear and slammed the door shut after them. The car leaped forward and tore into the street, careening wildly as it turned on two wheels. Satan lifted the tube that connected with Kayo in the driver's seat.

"You know the next stop," he barked. "What happened, Kayo?"

"Some guy sneaked into the alley from the street," Kayo reported. "He didn't see me. Probably he'd seen you and Slim, Cap'n, and figured you were alone. He watched after you for some time, when you went over the fence. He started to follow, so I climbed down and covered him.

"But he went for his gat anyway, cursing and swearing to beat the band."

Satan thought a moment. "He's not a railroad detective, or he would have closed right in."

Kayo yanked the wheel of the car hard, brought it to the curb, snapped off the lights. Several blocks ahead and on the opposite side of the avenue a squad car was roaring along, it's motor wide open. He started up again when the police car had swept by.

Three more calls the crew leader made on names that he had on his list… the list of the freight crew that had come east with the mystery train. But now Satan and Slim drew the shades of each room they entered. They weren't taking any more chances on being surprised by the watchful railroad detectives.

But each of the three calls were unavailing. The men knew no more of their strange trip than had the first man they had questioned. In every case, it was the same….

"… The freight was nearing Tonopah, Nevada." That was the last any of them knew before they came upon Jersey City. A distance of close to three thousand miles.

"No memory of the trips at all!" Satan marveled, as they sped to the next address on the list. "Not one of them!"

But at the next stop, it was different.

A SLOW-EYED, slow-voiced man sat up in answer to their shaking.

He sat cautiously still in bed, licked his lips nervously when Satan put his questions to him. Then:

"I—I'm not supposed to speak," he said, slowly, under Slim's prodding. "But you guys have got me on a spot. I don't want to die!"

"Then, talk!"

"Okay. At Tonopah, the yard bulls boarded the train and gave us all orders not to crack a word. We were transferred to a roundabout route and slammed through to Jersey City, running only at night. We got to Jersey City two days ago, and moved the freight onto a column of trucks to be run to the firm that had ordered the stuff."

Satan's eyes gleamed in the light of the flash. "We're finally getting someplace," he murmured. To the man: "If you know what's good for you, you'll give us the lowdown on what's back of this!"

The man squirmed a moment, seemed uneasy. "Well—" He stopped, closed his lips stubbornly. Slim prodded him with his automatic. "The inside dope is that there's a shipping union war on, an' the rebels in the line-up are cracking down on freight that is hard to replace."

Satan's eyes were bright in the dim light. "What's the rest of it? Who are the bosses in this racket? How is it the manufacturers are keeping their mouths shut, instead of squawking to the Feds?"

The man stared into the ray of the flashlight with shrewd eyes. "Then—you're not Sams in disguise? You're not Federal men just putting on an act?"

Satan's voice was hard when he spoke. "What gave you that idea?"

The railroad man shrugged. "I just heard that the Government was interested. One of the lads at the yard said so."

Satan stared a moment. Then: "Who are the bosses? And why do the roads keep quiet about this thing?"

"I dunno the bosses." He appeared to consider a moment. "Maybe the roads ain't peeping because they're afraid they'll scare a lot of express and freight out of their cars and onto the trucking systems."

Satan stood silent several minutes, turning the thing over in his mind. At length, he motioned to Slim. "Let's go. We've got all the dope we want for the time being." He made a motion toward his arm holster and swung for the door as Slim preceded him.

But instead of stepping out, he pivoted in a full turn, snapped his Satan flashlight into the darkness that had come over the room when Slim had deadened his own light.

The man in the bed was now out of it, standing in a half crouch—*and with a heavy automatic in his hand!*

But his lips curled back from his teeth in terror at the silhouetted figure that was on the glass of that flash… a figure that grew terrifyingly and into giant stature on the wall of the place, a figure of a horned and hooded Satan with pitchfork raised menacingly.

"Satan!" the man croaked in terror. His arm seemed stricken with paralysis as he struggled to get the automatic up. *"Captain— Satan!"* With a moan, he wrenched his arm up suddenly.

Two shots crashed deafeningly in the small room. Satan staggered slightly, steadied, pulled the trigger of his gun once again.

The man in front of him slammed back against the wall as the heavy slug caught him squarely in the chest. He slid to the floor... lifeless, but propped into a sitting position against the side of the bed.

Satan stooped, drew his device on the man's forehead with a piece of heavy black crayon.

Doors were opening in the hall of the place when the two went for the stairs. Slim, his dark eyes threatening in the slits of the mask, waved the aroused roomers back behind closed doors with his automatic. Satan went down the stairs three at a time, taking the steep risers at breakneck speed but with the surefootedness of a mountain goat. In a moment they were in the car.

The powerful machine slid away from the hotel and sped around a corner. Slim breathed with relief and sat back.

"Phew! That was close, Captain. How did you figure that guy out—and get him on the draw?"

Satan's face was inscrutable. "How do you think, Slim?"

The leader's lieutenant thought for several minutes as the car sped through the gray dawn. "Because he thought we were Sams?"

Satan shook his head. "No. Because all the others, Slim, had the self-same story. All had, in some mysterious way, lost their memories at Tonopah—excepting this fellow. And of all of them, he seemed the least scared. *Why?*"

Slim scratched an ear. "I give it up."

"Because," Satan pointed out, "this fellow had been *told* that the F.B.I. was investigating it—and he didn't fear us because his leader doesn't fear the Feds. Get it?"

"Good figuring, Captain," Slim agreed. "But how about the loss of memory business?"

"The same reasoning there," Satan pointed out. "He gave us a cock-and-bull story about hearing the F.B.I. was in it… yet he claims to know what the mystery was all about. The story doesn't hang together. If the railroad people know all about it, and if he remembers the trip, then why are the detectives watching him and why don't the rest break under pressure?"

"So where does that get us, Captain?"

Satan stared out the window of the speeding car a moment. Then he shook his head.

"I'm damned if I know, Slim. It doesn't get us any further than we were before. Only, we know that someone in that mystery train crew was planted there!"

Slim was staring at him in speculation when his eyes went suddenly wide with horror. A thin trickle of red crept from under Satan's black hat down his cheek and into the collar of his black shirt.

"Cap'n! You're wounded!"

"Just a crease," Satan shrugged. But there were faint white lines of weakness about his mouth. He rested his head against the back of the seat and his eyes went shut. Slim jumped for the speaking tube.

"Full speed for headquarters, Kayo!" he snapped. "The Captain has been shot!"

CHAPTER 6
A DEAD WIRE

SATAN OPENED his eyes to find Slim, Kayo and Doc bending over him. He blinked, turned his puzzled gaze around him. An expression of relief eased his drawn face.

"I guess that slug stunned me," he murmured. He made an effort to sit up, but Doc checked him with a gentle hand.

"Take it easy, Cap'n," the medical member of the crew advised. "I'm going to give you some stuff that'll pep you up. But you'd better rest a few minutes, first."

Satan nodded. But his eyes were eager. "What did you find out, Doc? Anything?"

Doc looked back at Satan steadily. "I don't know. I found a man who had been shot through the forehead. And in a number of other places, too. This much is definite: he *was* shot through the forehead twice, by identical bullets—forty-fives. The corpse was picked up on the lower East Side. It had been taken direct to the Morgue."

"Tried to make it look like a gang killing, eh? You printed the corpse?"

Doc shook his head. "Couldn't. His hands had been cut off."

"Any of the local police have an idea about him?"

"No. So far as I can learn, he's a stranger."

Slim drew a sudden breath. Satan's eyes went narrow. "We're up against a pretty vicious mob. One that will stop at nothing to hide its identity." The leader paused, his eyes thoughtful. "Slim, I want you to get in touch with the members of the crew

46

that you can reach now and tell them to be doubly cautious. I have a hunch that we're running into something so weird that it's… *uncanny!*"

"Right, Captain."

"And, Slim. Tell Solly when he goes to that Hassem Company office to try for prints of any kind that he can find."

"Right, Captain."

Doc mixed Satan a restorative, but the leader pushed the glass of medicine aside and got to his feet. "I don't need things like that, Doc," he said quietly. "I'll take a cold shower and let Kayo give me a rubdown. That's all I need."

The animal vitality poured back into Satan's heavily muscled, slim-hipped frame. He took a hot and then a cold shower in the baths with which the big warehouse room was equipped.

After a brisk rub by Kayo, the crew leader dressed in a fresh set of black clothes. He dismissed Doc and Slim, retired to a desk, where he spread a map of the United States. On the wall in front of him he pinned a railroad map of the country.

For some time he sat, marking with colored pins the positions that had been reported for the mystery train in the New York yards. He studied especially the terrain of the country near Tonopah, Nevada.

His brows were bent in deep thought when Slim answered the door in response to a code knock. It was Solly.

"Oi, Cap'n," the 'buyer' greeted his leader. "Them Hassem people ain't in beesness. They looked me over like I was a strange fish, and then they told me they're all sold up for three months."

"You saw Hassem?"

"Himself, Cap'n."

"Was he alone?"

"He was, Cap'n. I seen that his desk had been polished in the last couple of hours, so I didn't try any tricks to get prints."

"Stand by for orders," Satan dismissed him.

In the early afternoon, Pat and The Dutchman reported back. "No luck," they told Slim. "Not even a buzz."

And then Gentleman Dan made his appearance. He came blandly, a smile on his masked features. Satan pinned him with an inquiring eye; but Gentleman Dan fumbled a moment with the rubber strap of his silk mask.

"I was slipping this on at the bottom step—as per orders—when a man stepped into the doorway and stared up at me. I had to snap it off again."

Satan frowned. "Is he still there?"

"No. I started down again, and he dusted out for all he was worth."

"Why didn't you follow him?"

Gentleman Dan shrugged. "Didn't have time. Probably just someone who picked out a wrong address. But I have to hurry. I've been promised a job."

"What?" Satan came to his feet with a jump. "By whom? Where?"

Gentleman Dan's eyes clouded. "The job is waiting at Denver," he said slowly. "But I don't know who is hiring me. I didn't see the man; but he gave me two hundred dollars for traveling money, and a five hundred dollar bonus for a quick start. I leave to-night!"

SATAN'S EYES glinted satisfaction.

"Give me the story. Quick!"

Gentleman Dan made it thorough.

"I put in for a job at the main offices, then came down to the freight yards and made out I was looking for a friend. I got inside and nosed around a bit. A yard bull found me and ran me out. After that, I went to a saloon where a lot of mugs hang out. It's right by the yards. I got into conversation with a guy in clothes that looked as if they'd seen a lot of railroading. But he said he'd never had a rail job in his life."

Gentleman Dan paused, drew out a cigarette case and selected a smoke. When he had it going, he puffed a leisurely cloud of smoke and took up his story.

"I let drop that I was one tough tomato and that I had to skip town," he said, a smile creasing his good-looking mouth. "Well, after a few rounds of beer, I went into the men's room. And this guy followed me and stuck a gun in my gut. He wanted to frisk me." The smile became a wide grin. "I said, 'Here's my wallet, mister!' Just as if I was afraid of him.

"The sucker let me get my gun out and I dropped him with it. When he came to, I slapped him around a bit and frisked *him*. He had two thousand bucks with him. I burned half of it right under his nose, as a lesson to him. Then I took his gat and left the place. Bit of luck that I was still thirsty and stopped in another place down the line."

"How is that?"

"I was sitting in a wall-booth, trying to figure what to do next, when a voice spoke over my head... 'Don't look around

49

or you'll be drilled! I heard you wanted a job. You've got it. You start for Denver to-night. Check in at Spoletti's saloon, down by the tracks, and tell the bartender *he's homely as a hyena.* That's all!' Then *this* plopped down on my table." Gentleman Dan pulled an envelope from his pocket and passed it to Satan.

The crew leader snapped, "Drop that! Damn it, Dan—how often do I have to tell you to fingerprint everything you get like that?"

Gentleman Dan grinned. "Here they are." He yanked his wallet out, extracted a sheet of paper and passed it. "I bought a camera, went to a hotel room, and made the sprints and snapped them before they'd faded out any."

Satan's eyes gleamed. "Good!" He turned. "Pat! You've got a connection at Police Headquarters? Get the dope on these. And rush!" He swung back to Gentleman Dan. "This man who tried to hold you up—what did he look like?"

"Oh, nothing unusual. Medium build, pale blue eyes, a hard mouth. But his hands were pretty clean for a freight-crew man. Smooth skin, nails unbroken. He's a gunner or I miss my guess."

"And carries plenty of money," Satan said slowly. "He's a phony, that much is sure. But how do we know he's with the gang we're after?"

"Only way to find out is to go to Denver," Slim said reluctantly. Gentleman Dan was a cool hand and Slim hated to spare him.

"Right," Satan agreed. "Of course, you'll use a false name, Dan?"

The man nodded. "Sure. Any special instructions, Cap'n?"

"No. Just handle yourself with kid gloves. And if this doesn't look like our set-up, dust out and fly back here immediately. If we've jumped out of the city to chase down any leads, go to your telephone and wait for a call from Slim."

"Right, Cap'n."

Satan stood, stuck out a browned hand. "Good luck, Dan."

After the man had gone, Satan turned to Slim. "I have a hunch that Dan has hit on something." But Slim didn't share his leader's elation.

"I have, too, Captain. And I have a hunch that trouble is in the air for all of us. I don't like the looks of this hokus-pokus at all!"

He liked it less an hour later, when Pat checked in again. They all went tense at the man's breathless entrance, his stiff-legged walk, the tight lines that widened his mouth.

"There's *three* sets of prints on the envelope," Pat reported. "One—'Larry The Dude' as they call him at Headquarters." Slim and Satan exchanged looks, the lieutenant smothering a grin. "Two—a guy called 'Doctor Vashter,' a medico with a criminal record who dropped out of sight twenty years ago. And third—"

The squat, powerful little Irishman paused and licked his lips. "The Saints save us, the third are those of Jake Largo, that warped devil who was killed twenty years ago!"

Slim whistled. "Remember what Soapy said when you described the man with the pop-eyes, Captain?"

Satan nodded. His eyes became a deeper gray as he stared hard at Pat. "That's impossible, Pat!"

The man shrugged. "Sure it is, Cap'n. An' sure I told them so. But—couldn't it be they are *like* Largo's? Or that in some way this mob is usin' a faked set o' prints to throw people off the track?"

Satan nodded. "It's been done." He considered a moment. "Pat, how long will it take you to check Vashter's record? His *complete* record?"

"An hour."

"Do it."

IT WAS dark when Satan sat over the written documents that revealed the criminal activities of the man Vashter. The crew started up suddenly when Satan came to his feet, his masked face tense.

"Slim! We've got something. Listen:"

He read:

"VASHTER, VASILI. Born October 10,1887. Emigrated from Russia with parents at age of fifteen years. Left home upon completion of medical studies. His father, an invalid chemist, died in poverty shortly after. His mother committed suicide."

"Nice guy," Slim commented shortly.

"Vashter war hired by the Great Eastern and Continental Railroad as a medical inspector. Was first brought to notice of police when accused of passing unfit men for bribes. Cleared of this charge, he was later assigned to check on injuries of passengers involved in wrecks.

"Convicted of conspiracy to defraud, he was sentenced to five years in jail. Upon his release, he posed as an insurance inspector of the medical staff, was convicted of securing releases for small sums, then selling these to the insurance companies for sums considerably greater.

"Vashter was sentenced to twenty years at hard labor. He had been

imprisoned this second time only four months when he killed two guards and escaped.

"*Wanted for first degree murder. Believed to have fled to Russia in 1918. Vashter is reputed to possess hypnotic powers.*"

Satan looked up, his eyes flashing.

Slim stared. "What's that last got to do with it?"

Satan was impatient. "Don't you see, Slim? Vashter is connected with railroads. He's shrewd, clever, but crooked as a mountain trail. Remember the men with the failing memories on this freight? Vashter is a hypnotist!"

Slim was doubtful. "Pretty hard to hypnotize a whole train crew for that length of time, Captain."

"We'll worry about that part of it later," Satan countered. "You agree Vashter has had the railroad experience to enable him to carry off a crime against the railroads? You agree that his prints were on that envelope Gentleman Dan got? You agree it's conceded he's still alive?"

Slim was not convinced. "What about this Jake Largo, Captain? His prints were on that paper, too. Yet, you remember he died twenty years ago, was shot through the brain?"

"I wasn't here twenty years ago," Satan said. "I was in Germa— er—I was abroad," he caught himself up.

"Largo hung on for several weeks after he was shot in a gambling scrape," Slim recalled the records. "He was a clever, daring gambler. But he palmed one ace too many. His mob offered a hundred thousand if some doctor could operate, could save him. But he died. Accounts of his funeral were in all the papers. He was cremated."

Satan said shortly, "Argue all you want, Slim! We're moving to find Vashter. Now, before we—"

The telephone buzzer sounded quietly in the large room. Slim went to the wall, opened a secret panel. He yanked out the cleverly concealed instrument. "Hello?" He listened, then turned to Satan.

"It's Hank. He's calling from San Francisco!"

Satan crossed with long strides to the telephone. "Right, Hank. What is it?"

He listened in silence for several minutes. Then his face went gray with sudden emotion. "What? What's that? An old buddy of yours working in the dispatch office tried to give you a bum steer? Yes. Yes. Told you finally to go *where?* My God, Hank— you mustn't listen to him! No, I tell you, *NO!*"

Satan fairly shouted the last into the instrument. Then he stared suddenly at the earpiece, clicked the connection vigorously. After a futile moment, he said, "Let it go, operator. My party was disconnected.... No... I don't think he'll call back!"

He shoved the 'phone back into the panel and turned with a grim face. "You heard? There was a dull thud, then the line went dead."

"What's up?" Slim whispered. "You think Hank—? You think something's wrong?"

"An old friend told Hank he was nuts," the leader said tonelessly. "Then, when Hank pressed him, he told him a secret... told him there was one man who could give him the dope, and that was *'The Hyena' at Spoletti's in Denver!* Said to have Hank tell him he was sent there by him to get the story."

54

"And the man, Captain? The man who told him?"

"Hank didn't say," Satan said slowly. "He didn't have time to say. Hank, I am afraid, was knocked kicking while he was talking to me."

"Cap'n," Doc barked suddenly. "How about Gentleman Dan?"

Satan's eyes bored into Slim. "You know what plane Dan took? The name he went under, on the train?"

Slim shook his head. "No, Captain."

"Damn it," Satan exploded. "I want to tip Dan off, tell him to find out who that dispatcher is. Until we know where Hank is, if he's dead or alive, we don't move another step after this mob!"

Slim shrugged. "The only thing we can do is to fly out there, nose around ourselves, Captain. There's no way to reach him by wire or 'phone."

"Right!" The leader turned, his hand raised. "Everybody get set for a flight to San Francisco… now! Slim! Get in touch with Soapy, tell him to meet us at the airport. We have just—" He paused, his head cocked. "What's that?"

A shuffling, rustling sound came from beyond the great iron door. Slim tiptoed close, stood with his head bent, his eyes alert. Then a sudden hammering came on the door and the smashing punch of a strong ram against it.

"Open up in the name of the Law!" a bellow came from the other side. "Federal Bureau of Investigation, Satan! We have the place surrounded. You can't get away!"

CHAPTER 7
THE DEATH TRAP

S ATAN AND his crew moved with the silence of trained men to the exact center of the room. Slim jumped to the wall, pressed against a panel. A small square of wood gave inward. Satan's lieutenant grasped the handle that was brought into view, twisted it to the right, snapped the panel shut again.

He raced to join the others as the pounding renewed. The heavy crash of the battering ram sounded again. Sirens screamed through the street outside, brakes squealed. Satan's face was grim.

"You've got it set for fifteen seconds, Slim?"

"Right, Captain." The men stood in a tight knot, shoulders touching. "It ought to—There it goes now!"

From the fissures at the base of the walls on all sides, jets of black smoke poured into the room. Simultaneously, there was a trembling of the floor where Satan and his crew stood.

Slowly, the flooring on which they stood dropped away... down... down... to the underground escape that Satan had provided for just such an emergency. As the hidden elevator carried them below the floor level, another square of wood, identical with the floor above and painstakingly contrived to dovetail perfectly, was released. It closed above their heads with a bang.

A tight smile twisted the corners of Satan's mouth.

"By the time the Sams get the tear gas and the smoke screen out of their eyes, we'll be miles away... and they won't know any more than they do now!"

The Dutchman blinked. "They will if they find that handle in the wall, Cap'n."

Slim explained. "The elevator has to be re-set before it can be used again. They can pull that handle until doomsday and the floor won't move."

"But the telephone? They'll find that and trace the connection, the call that came from San Francisco, too."

Satan flashed his lamp into the jet darkness as the hidden elevator stopped. "That telephone is a tapped-in line, connecting with a telephone in an empty office in another street. When that office 'phone rings, our buzzer sounds. Now—" he crossed to a wall in the damp cellar that was several stories underground, yanked at the wires that stretched up through the flooring above—"we take these wires out and they have nothing."

Satan coiled the wires into a tight ring. Slim stood waiting by the far wall. Nearby, a roar started up and a heavy rumble filled the place. When it had died, Slim opened a floor trap and yanked a lever. A section of the cellar wall swung open, revealing the gleaming metal of tracks.

"San Francisco is our destination," Satan said, his voice suddenly flat and commanding. "You men change to your regular clothes, get planes out of here as soon as possible. We meet at midnight tomorrow in 'Frisco, at the S.D. & R. freight yards. Understood?"

"Right, Cap'n," the men answered soberly.

"This escape of ours leads into the new subway," Satan went on. "There's a station just below us… to the left. Another is seven blocks to the right. You men will go singly, taking off your masks as you start up the tracks. That'll keep you from seeing one another face to face. The first man will start to the right, the next to the left. At an interval of two minutes, the next pair starts, right and left. Got it?"

"Right, Cap'n."

"Okay. Solly and The Dutchman first. Start!"

In six minutes, Satan's crew had cleared into the subway tunnel, two trains roaring by in the interval. Slim and Satan waited until they had all made their escape, then followed, heading for the nearest exit.

"You get Soapy," Satan told his lieutenant as they went quickly down the tracks. "Meet me at the airport for the night plane."

"What do you plan to do in San Francisco, Cap'n?" Slim asked.

"To find out if Hank has been murdered," was the grim answer. "If he hasn't, then Gentleman Dan isn't safe, may walk right into a death trap at Spoletti's. Hank is a new man, may not be able to stand the torture that this gang will put to him— may give out the information that I'm trying to plant men in that gang!"

"That's right," Slim remembered. "Hank was there when you gave Dan and Pat and The Dutchman their instructions. How about sending Soapy to Spoletti's in Denver—to see if he can spot Gentleman Dan, warn him?"

Satan shook his head slowly, "No, Slim. In the first place, Dan was careless and let somebody tail him to our headquarters. Remember? He spoke of someone looking up the stairs after him when he came back from the yards?"

Slim was grave. "By God, that's right! And that's where the F.B.I. mob got the tip-off on us! Whoever followed Dan knew he was one of the Satan crew—and relayed the tip to the F.B.I.!"

Satan nodded. "Hoping to get us out of the way. So—Dan is either safe, or he isn't. There's no helping that now. Dan will have to walk into his death trap and beat the game as best he can. If someone is watching Dan, they'd spot Soapy if he went to help Dan."

Both men were sober as they unmasked and went up the platform steps. Gentleman Dan was a favorite of the crew, and they were saddened by the peril that he faced.

But Satan's activities were work that would make the Devil himself flinch; and Satan's crew, one and all, knew the fate that awaited them if they were uncovered in their jobs.

"Poor Dan," Slim said in a husky voice as they separated.

THE STEELY-EYED, plainly dressed man at the very rear of the big transport plane attracted the interest of the pretty little hostess more than once on the voyage.

He sat with his face shaded from the view of the other passengers and poured over maps through most of the trip. Once, the girl came near and suggested, "Would you care for a pot of tea, sir? Or a cup of coffee?"

"No!"

The girl started with the intensity of that low voice. Satan looked up quickly, the stern lines of his face softening into a smile. "I'm sorry, miss. No—thank you! I'm very busy."

The hostess made her way up the aisle, paused at the front to speak with a gaunt, morose looking individual who, unlike

Satan, couldn't seem to get enough attention. Satan's face flashed the ghost of a grin.

Midway up the aisle, a jolly-faced, fat, well-dressed man, his hair as blond as that of the hostess, stared at the morose man up forward with plain envy. He beamed when the girl looked his way, her face flushing when she caught those worshipful blue eyes on her.

Directly across the aisle from the fat man, a small, wiry chap with a large hooked nose glowered at the male flirt. "Oi, what a racket!" he muttered. "I'm dying of thirst and not even water she offers *me!*"

Satan dropped his eyes to his maps again.

At San Francisco, Satan sat quiet while the others hurried off. Then he came slowly down the aisle. The hostess, her duties to the passengers discharged, was coming back into the plane.

"Miss," Satan addressed himself to her mildly, "can you tell me the quickest route to the S.D. & R. freight yards?"

The girl flashed him a warm smile. "Why, of course I can. My father and brother work for the company." She gave Satan quick, accurate directions. She refused the tip Satan offered… politely. But her eyes were on guard when she saw the size of the bill he held out. A tiny frown creased her forehead.

"What is your father's name?" Satan asked casually. "Maybe I know him. What department is he in?"

The girl was suddenly cold, aloof. She indicated the name-plate badge that she wore over her left breast pocket. *Miss Sonya Kerstadt*, it read. "His name is the same as mine, naturally."

Satan thanked her suavely. But he hadn't missed the sudden

Suddenly the shadow
of Satan appeared.

fear in the girl's eyes, her desperate effort to seem standoffish. When he came down the debarking-ladder, he ran squarely into the fat, blond man who had stared at the girl so admiringly throughout the trip.

Satan's eyes were hard and he jostled the man severely. But the jolly one didn't notice. His eyes were all for Miss Sonya Kerstadt, the hostess of the big plane.

He boarded a taxi, but instead of going to the freight yards, he went directly to the telephone building in the heart of the city. He got there just before closing time.

He flashed a badge on a minor official seated at a desk. "I'm an F.B.I. man," he explained. "There was a call made from San Francisco last night that I want to trace. I want to know where that call was made from. It was a long distance call to New York."

The executive stared, seemed about to speak. But Satan's eyes weren't inviting either confidences or questions. "What is the number that was called?"

Satan passed him a slip of paper with the number written on it. The man went into a huddle with another executive. Both looked at Satan furtively. Satan cleared his throat harshly and the two men hurried down a lane of desks, disappeared through a door. Almost casually, Satan unbuttoned his coat, let his hand rest near the left lapel.

But there was no trick to it. His man was back in five minutes with the information. "There's the number that called." He passed an address to Satan.

Satan didn't even look at it. "It's near the freight yards," he said in a dreamy voice, his eyes piercing the man. "It's a rough section of town. It's probably a restaurant… and saloon… and it's a coin machine."

"Say!" the telephone executive breathed admiringly. "You Federal men certainly know your stuff!"

SATAN WENT directly to the freight yards. He dismissed his cab a block away and faded into a darkened hallway. He watched down the street for some time before he went nearer.

Finally, when he was sure that there was no one watching the particular street he was on, Satan went quickly along the building line and turned. He found himself confronted by a high, iron picket fence. He sized up the ground on the other side… a narrow ledge. He placed one hand on the bar between the pickets and scaled the fence lightly, twisting in midair to come down close to the fence on the other side.

It was a drop of some fifteen feet to the tracks. Satan glanced about to see if he were being watched, then took from his pocket a length of thin, almost incredibly strong rope made of giraffe's hide. He made a doubled line of it, secured it to a paling in the fence, slid quickly down to the tracks and rolled the thong-rope up to stick it back into his pocket. He walked down the high wall at the side of the maze of tracks until he came to a line of freight cars. He doubled out past these, went along close to them, crossed again. There was a crunch of heavy shoes on the cinders close by, and Satan bent and crawled under a car. The steps came louder, passed, died in the distance. Satan came out and walked quickly down the tracks again. He halted suddenly at a low whistle… muffled, but close by. The door of a box car was open by the merest crack.

"Ess—em," a soft voice called. "Ess—em."

"Slim!" Satan glanced quickly up and down, then vaulted lightly up to the floor of the car through the opening Slim made for him. The door shut again.

Satan flashed his cigarette lighter alive to light a smoke. Then he reversed the barrel-shaped object of enamel-and-gold, bringing a weird, bluish, Satan-silhouetted light on the faces of the men gathered in the car.

"Slim— Pat— Doc— Soapy— Kayo— Solly—" he paused, his eyes going hard on the last of the group—"and The Dutchman!"

The big man moved uneasily under Satan's scrutiny and the pitiless glare of that light. "Dutchman." Satan said, his lips thin and his voice hard, "the next time you loaf on the job to give a girl the eye, it's going to go hard with you!"

The blond crew man flushed guiltily. "Gee, Cap'n!" His voice was awed, husky. "I—I only stayed a minute. Just long enough to ask how long she would be in town. How—how did you find out?"

"I know every move you men make," Satan answered, his voice brittle. "Let that be a lesson to you two new men—to you and Solly. This is your second—er—*trip* with me. It'll be your last if you don't keep to your business. It may be the last for all of us, if you don't keep your wits about you and your thoughts on what's ahead of us."

"I'm—sorry," The Dutchman said, his face sheepish. "It didn't do any good, anyway. The gal turned on the ice water and frosted me."

There was a chuckle in the darkness behind Satan. The leader's flash swung, pinned Slim.

"Laugh hard, Slim," he snapped, his voice savage. "Hank has walked into a trap right here in this city! Gentleman Dan, as we all know, walked into another death trap in Denver... *The Hyena's trap!*

"And right this minute, you and I are leaving the boys here—to walk into the identical trap that Hank was in when he called us on the telephone!" He swung his light again, his voice harsh.

"You men wait here for some word from us... for two hours! If we're not back by that time, your orders are to go to Spoletti's in Denver and clean the place out. Then—disband!"

Doc blinked. His calm voice was faintly questioning. "We're not to wait for you—here?"

"If Slim and I aren't back in two hours." Satan said slowly, "We'll *never* be back!"

He opened the door enough to peer out, then dropped noiselessly down onto the cinders. Slim followed. The door of the box car slid shut again and Satan's crew sat down to commence the grim, two-hour vigil.

CHAPTER 8
SATAN TAKES COMMAND

THE PLACE Satan sought was only a few blocks from the freight depot. The leader walked rapidly, silently—his eyes hard and his mouth thin, until Slim spoke.

"What do you make of this 'Hyena' angle, Captain?"

"A fanciful name that some mob leader has given himself. It's plain he's the man we're after. First, Gentleman Dan got those instructions… *'Tell the bartender he's homely as a hyena.'* Obviously a password. Hank's man just as obviously sent him into what was planned to be a trap—by telling him to *ask* for The Hyena."

"And then knocked him off while he was relaying the information to you?"

Satan nodded. "I'm afraid so." He shook his head somberly. "You remember, Slim, that Dan got the password *before* he was tracked to our hideout? The man who followed him probably spotted him in the act of slipping on his mask, made the deduction that he was one of Satan's Crew."

Slim was grave. "And, by now, The Hyena knows that Dan is on his way, is waiting for him! And poor Gentleman Dan thinks everything is all right."

Satan rounded a corner, his eyes alert and studying the district. "We are in a risky game, Slim. Dan knows better than to let himself be tracked. And that's the danger. One slip… one careless moment… and the entire crew will be blown higher than the stars." His voice was sorrowful. "Gentleman Dan dug his own pit. He'll have to climb clear of it himself, or wait— if he can—until I have tracked down Hank, found out what happened to him—and get the man who gave him that bum steer."

They came abreast of a grimy-windowed, dimly lit restaurant-saloon. Satan hardly seemed to look as he walked rapidly by. At the corner, he stopped Slim. "Seven men at the bar," he said tersely. "One bartender on duty—a big, tough-looking man. And in the corner near the telephone booth, a husky, blond lad of about twenty-five. I'll go in first, Slim. You wait five minutes, then follow.

"When you come in, walk right up to me and say: *'I couldn't find him around the yards.'* I'll do the rest." To Slim's perplexed look, he added, "I got the name of a man working for the railroad. I can talk loud enough to let them overhear, in there—make them think we're just casual visitors looking for a friend."

"Okay." Slim bared his wristwatch. "I'll stall here for five minutes. Captain."

Satan pushed open the door of the saloon and walked in. A silence fell over the place. The bartender looked quickly, then away again. But the crew leader was aware of the eyes of the others on him in the mirror. He ranged up to the bar, letting his eyes barely flick over the man near the telephone.

But his muscles went tense at the savage look that the burly youth in that chair was bending on him… a look of suspicion that burned in those pale eyes, was made threatening by the ugly curve of the brutal mouth.

"Scotch and water," he said flatly. He grimaced at the rot-gut brand on the bottle that was set before him. But he poured a stiff slug of the stuff, downed the fiery liquid at a gulp. He poured a second, a third drink. He pushed the water away from him roughly.

"That'll be forty-five cents, stranger," the big bartender said.

Satan stuffed a hand into his pants pocket and hauled out a

wad of bills big as his fist. He selected a twenty and threw it to the wide-eyed bartender. "Buy the house a drink," he ordered.

The saloon-keeper eyed the twenty suspiciously... but he made change, started to set up the drinks for the eight occupants, and one for himself. A surly voice raised behind Satan.

"I'll buy me own drinks, Pete. Tell yer dude customer he ain't the big shot he thinks he is!"

The bartender looked at Satan nervously. The crew leader gave no more attention to the sullen man near the telephone booth than if he hadn't spoken. Instead, he was examining the bills he had got in change for his twenty.

He pushed a bill toward the barkeep. "Not a bad job, this," he drawled. "Couldn't do much better myself. But the green your man used is a shade too bright. Tell him to mix a little more black with it next time."

Down the bar, a man sucked in his breath loudly. But Satan was pushing another bill across the mahogany. "Now—this five-spot, this 'fin'—don't you know any better than to put Lincoln's face on it? Save Lincoln for the one-dollar bills... if you go in for that petty racket. And the number *five* in the upper left corner looks like it's been used for a fish hook!"

The bartender's face had gone pasty. His meaty hand was dropping from the bar... reaching down behind it. An ugly automatic seemed to grow suddenly in Satan's right hand. "Hold it!" he snapped. "You cheap, fuddle-brained clown! What are you trying to pull? Get some dough up there on the counter—the real McCoy this time!—or I'll pick your teeth for you with my little lead splinters."

His eyes raised to the mirror in back of the saloon keeper. They narrowed to mere slits. "Back in your chair, you! *Now!* Or I'll put a slug into that unmannerly puss of yours."

The sullen blond giant near the booth sank slowly back into the chair from which he had risen so stealthily. The bar-keep blinked, cleared his throat, managed a sickly grin.

"You're purty slick, pardner," he said shakily. "Put away that boom-boom before I shake myself clean out of my shoes!"

The latch of the door clicked. Everybody turned.

Slim came in slowly, his eyes sizing up the situation. He backed up against the door and flashed a gun from his arm holster, another from his left hip. Satan grinned.

"Don't get excited, Slim," he drawled. "Just a couple of playful boys in here that I had to set down. Put away your cannons. They're not tough—not even a little!"

SLIM SLID his artillery out of sight again. He walked over slowly, said in a mild voice: "I couldn't find him around the yards."

Satan shook his head as if in anger. "Why the hell didn't—" he paused, his eyes hard as they swept the listening men, forced their faces away—"why didn't our pal give us his home address! Now we gotta call the Line up, and you know how much I like that. What if they were to trace the call?"

Slim played his part. "Who can tell you at the office?"

Satan's smile was crafty. "I'm not telling all I know! Not to the mugs in this or any other place."

He walked to the telephone booth and closed the door carefully. Slim took a position where he could watch every man in the place. Satan's voice came clear and loud through the thin partitions.

"Hello?… S.D. & R.?… I'm trying to get in touch with a friend of mine…. Yeah…. That's right…. No, he don't work there; not *regularly!* But you got a man named—" Satan paused—"Kerstadt, who will know where I can get him. Can you tell me where I can get Kerstadt?"

He paused a moment, glanced quickly out at Slim. The gaunt man was tense, his hand creeping toward his lapel again. Satan sensed something had gone wrong, made the rest of it quick….

"…You *won't* give me any information? O.K.—and thanks just the same!" He dropped the receiver on the hook and came out of the booth warily.

But Slim had relaxed again, was leaning up against the bar. Satan ranged over by his side, spilled his drink in the spittoon when he had a chance.

"The blond mug by the booth nearly went through the roof when you were talking!" Slim spoke softly through stiff lips.

Satan frowned. "That's funny. The only reason I used the name Kerstadt was because it would stand a check-up. The hostess on the plane, remember? That's her name, and her father works for the S.D. & R. But they wouldn't know him *here.* Not *that* kid's old man!"

Slim straightened, half-turned. "Here comes that guy now! Watch it, Captain!"

But the blond giant's face was guileless, his manner detached. He put his foot on the bar rail and leaned near Satan.

"Who wants Kerstadt?"

70

"Who wants to know!"

The man nodded to the bartender, accepted Satan's previous offer of a drink. He drained the pony of whiskey at a gulp, wiped his mouth with a hairy hand. "Kerstadt wants to know," he answered slowly. "That's my name."

Satan controlled the start of surprise that the answer gave him. This thug—related to that girl on the transport plane. His mind raced over the thing. "Her father and brother, she said, worked for the railroad. This must be the brother." But he didn't open his mouth.

The ruse had the desired effect. Kerstadt moved nearer. "I'm giving you the straight goods," he said from the corner of his mouth. "You from the East?"

Still Satan didn't move a muscle. He and Slim stood as unmoving as statues, their eyes veiled, their faces hard. The blond licked his lips. "I know. You want the old man, don't you? Well, he's skipped—taken a two weeks vacation that he had coming to him." He paused and laughed harshly. "I don't think the old boy will show back at all, though."

"He'd better!" Satan growled when the man fell silent. "If he knows what's good for him, he'll show back here again!"

The younger Kerstadt batted his eyes and stared around furtively. "I can take you to him," he said. "You don't understand, but he can't show around here till a certain stink dies down. I—can't tell you why!"

Satan's thoughts raced like wildfire, around and around, trying to set the thing straight in his mind. "This is the place that Hank called me from—where Hank was ganged up," he reasoned. "Kerstadt, here, is a tough egg… no matter what his sister is! And the father is in it, too. The father is older, would be about Hank's age. Evidently, he hung out in here, too, until—" The leader dropped his eyes to his cigarette case, kept them veiled from young Kerstadt.

"He hung out here—*until Hank made that call!*"

He puffed on his smoke for several minutes, then turned to the man on his left. "I'll play with you, youngster," he said thinly, his eyes hard and the cigarette hanging from his lips. "But," he added, with an evil smile that brought a shudder to Kerstadt's frame, "if you don't play nice, you'll never play anywhere again this side of Hell! Lead the way!"

The barkeep sighed audible relief when Satan's eyes raked him for the last time and the gray-eyed leader stepped through the door into the growing dusk.

Kerstadt walked nervously, his eyes watchful. Every now and then he looked back over his shoulder. He led the two several blocks straight on, then turned to go a like distance to his left. He halted near an old-fashioned, brownstone house. "This is it."

Satan said casually to Slim, "Go back and get our car and drive it up here." He winked covertly.

"The baggage, too?"

"Everything!" Satan was satisfied that Slim understood, would bring the crew.

Young Kerstadt's eyes narrowed. He clipped, "Say, what is this? Neither of you guys is going anyplace, see? You springing a trap on us? I thought you were the real goods!"

"Go ahead, Slim." Satan turned, his gun in his hand suddenly.

72

"Get along, you! One peep out of you and I'll blow your top into a sewer. And no tricks! Just one bad move— just one, mind you!— and you'll quit worrying about anything."

The Mark of Satan

As Kerstadt started slowly up the stoop, Satan chuckled. "I told you I'd play with you. But I play pretty rough when people try any funny stuff with me!"

He stood, watchful, as Kerstadt fumbled in his pockets; but it was only for a key. The blond giant slipped the thing in the door and turned it.

Satan stepped into the dark hall after him and the door closed again.

CHAPTER 9
THE SWEDE TALKS TO DEATH

THERE WAS utter silence for a moment, then a scraping, shuffling sound. A beam of light jumped alive in Satan's hand. "Hold it," the crew leader snapped.

Young Kerstadt had been making a stealthy way through the

dark to the staircase that climbed up out of the dreary hall. Now he stopped, his eyes desperate. Satan coolly estimated the youth.

"Don't push your luck too far," he warned. "My finger might just slip and then it'd be too bad! Where's your father?"

"I—don't know." Kerstadt's eyes were frightened… but they peered wonderingly at the beam of light—the fine, strong beam that shone down the blue barrel of Satan's automatic.

Satan smiled slightly. "Neat trick, eh? A flash on the gun barrel! It helps you to see… *and* to aim. For instance—" he raised the gun until the narrow ray pierced Kerstadt's right eye. Now, if I were to squeeze this trigger just a *little* harder—!"

"I'll crack!" the husky blond whispered brokenly. "I'll take you to Big Sven." He sensed Satan's question, hurried to explain. "That's what they call my father—Big Sven."

"Get going," Satan ordered. He followed close on the man's heels as the youth led the way up one flight of stairs, then turned at the landing and started for the third floor. A door at the top opened slightly, throwing a shaft of light onto the stairs.

"Who is dot?" a guttural voice called—a voice in which Satan recognized sheer terror. The crew leader pressed his gun into the small of young Kerstadt's back. The blond shivered; but he got the idea.

"It's me, Dad," he answered in a shaky voice.

"Oh! It's you, Ole!" There was displeasure in that greeting. But Satan wasn't stopping to measure that, to figure its significance, now. He prodded the slow moving youth up, through the door. Big Sven Kerstadt's eyes started with terror when he saw Satan.

He tried to slam the door shut, but Satan kicked it wide, stepped into the room and slammed the door behind. He felt the key in the lock, twisted it without turning, slipped the metal thing into his pocket.

He sized up Big Sven at a glance, waved the son, Ole, over near the elder. "Must be six-four," Satan judged. "Built like a powerhouse. But he's frightened... badly frightened." He shifted his eyes to a door at his right.

"What's that? Where does that lead?"

Big Sven licked his lips. "It's—a closet. Who bane you, mister?"

Satan ignored the question. He sniffed the air of the room, then bent a hard look on the older man. "Who is in there?"

"Nobody." The big fellow shifted nervously. "Bane nobody, no time."

"You lie!" The words crackled like a whiplash. "There's cigarette smoke in this room." His eyes drifted to the pipes that were on a small table next to a tobacco bowl. "And you smoke pipes," he added slowly.

Big Sven was frantic. "Ay bane tell you truth. Bane nobody in dot closet!"

Satan's face was grim. "Well, in that case, it isn't going to hurt if I blow a few holes through that door." He raised his gun slowly. Ole stood his ground. But Big Sven jumped to the door, barred it with his body.

"No, no! Pliss, mister, don't shoot—don't shoot! Bane nobody in dot closet!" Beads of perspiration stood out on the big fellow's face, and his eyes pleaded piteously, blue eyes that were frantic, crazed.

And then it came… a voice that rocked Satan back on his heels and paralyzed those other two men into statues….

"Open the door, father! Stand away! I'll come out. I have nothing to be afraid of." But there was a tremor in that high, brave, girlish voice that gave the lie to the words.

Big Sven sobbed brokenly and stepped to one side. The door came open slowly.

It was Sonya Kerstadt… the hostess from the airliner.

HER FACE was pale, drawn, and her eyes wide. The pupils dilated at sight of Satan. "You!"

Satan smiled grimly. "No one else," he said amiably. "What are you doing in the closet?"

Sonya Kerstadt flushed. "I don't see that it's your business what I do in my father's house."

Satan's smile died. "Maybe the airline officials might like to know what went on in this house." He saw the quick look that Sonya directed at her father, and the older man's painful flush and averted face.

Ole chipped in with, "You know this man, Sonya? From where? Who is he?" His voice was brittle, eager. Satan let the girl answer.

"I never saw him until he got on the transport yesterday, Ole. *And he asked about you and father!*" The girl's eyes were bright, accusing. "He wanted to know where the S.D. & R. yards were."

Satan was amused at the girl's misinterpretation of his casual question about her family—when he merely had asked for directions to the freight yards. But he kept his eyes alert on Ole.

The younger man was nervous; but plainly calculating. Satan had caught the slight, sidling movements with which he was edging back toward the windows at the rear of the room. But he said nothing to him.

Big Sven fought for composure. "Vot you vant—you?" he growled beligerently at Satan. "Vot you do, huh? Vy you come here?"

Satan cocked his head; but he answered steadily. "I'm here to find Hank," he said evenly. "And don't try to run any ringers on me, Big Sven—or you'll find yourself mussed up a bit and behind bars!"

The blood drained from the man's face again. Ole cursed slowly and with imagination until Satan pinned him with a hard eye. Then he stood rooted where he was, his breath coming hard, his eyes frantic. But the crew leader was listening again.

There were sounds on the steps outside. Then a low, musical whistle.

"Who?" Satan asked in a low, deadly voice.

"Ess-em," came the soft answer.

Satan flipped the key from his pocket and held it out to the girl.

"Open that door," he said. "You have nothing to fear, so long as you don't try any rough stuff." Then, when she hesitated, *"Jump to it!"*

Sonya bridled and took the key. "You don't have to yell at me," she said with defiant eyes. But she gasped the next moment

77

Deliberately Satan
pulled the trigger.

when Slim, masked and with his automatic in his hand, drifted into the room.

"The boys are coming now, Captain," he whispered. "I'm stationing Kayo at the front door and Soapy out back, on guard."

"Good!" Satan whipped his silk mask from his pocket, snapped it over his eyes. "Let them come, Slim."

Satan's lieutenant stepped through the door again, disappeared down the stairs. Sonya Kerstadt tried to look mildly amused; but there was fright in her eyes.

"What is this, a game?" she asked in a shaky voice. "Why do you come in here unmasked, and then suddenly decide to hide your features?"

Satan's eyes were slits of gray in that silk covering. "Because," he said slowly, his voice low and vibrant, "Captain Satan and his men appear in whatever way I choose. I'm sorry you disapprove."

Ole Kerstadt's eyes went wide, bulged horribly. His mouth worked in a frenzy as he tried to force words that didn't want to come. "And you—? You are—?"

"*I — am — Captain — Satan!*"

Young Kerstadt screamed his terror, took two steps in Satan's direction. The leader waved his gun menacingly. But the blond giant was insane with fear. He ripped at the buttons of his shirt, plunged a hand in and tugged.

"Keep away from that gun!" Satan barked. "Kerstadt! You hear me? *Drop it!*"

But the youth ignored the threat, was ripping his automatic from its concealment under his shirt. His hand came out, his arm started to level.

Satan sighed and pressed the trigger. A deafening crash sounded in the room and a heavy body thudded to the floor. Sonya stared unbelievingly a moment, then screamed with hysteria. Big Sven collapsed into a chair, his head in his hands. Ole thrashed with his legs twice, spasmodically, then lay still.

"*Ya, ya,*" the big man muttered. "He's dead, my Ole. *Ya,* it is better so!"

The door burst open and Satan's crew surged in with guns drawn, their eyes hard. They stopped at sight of the dead man on the floor. Satan shook his head slowly.

"I warned him that if he tried any tricks, he'd find I played hard!"

Sonya faced Satan, her eyes blazing. "You murderer!" she flared. "Oh, you despicable, low, horrible—"

Satan murmured, "I'm sorry you had to see this, Miss Kerstadt. But—" he indicated the father with his head—"I think you know your brother was a criminal and mixed up in a very dangerous, serious racket."

The girl bit her lip. "Oh, that's your alibi, is it? Because my step-brother was involved with bad company, you take it on yourself to kill him!"

Big Sven was staring at his daughter, his eyes heavy. Satan sensed that the man thought he knew plenty of whatever racket his son had been mixed in. He stayed silent, signaled his men not to speak. The big railroad man opened his hands in a simple gesture of resignation.

"Sonya!" His voice was broken, almost a sob. "It is true. My Ole vas already bad. He vas crooked, und made me giff him information dot he used vit dot gang he knew." He flinched at the dumb pain that was in the girl's eyes. "I—I couldn't tell you, my Sonya. I couldn't bring shame on you, like it vas on me."

Satan crossed to the big fellow, laid a sympathetic hand on his shoulder. "Big Sven," he said slowly, "I had to kill Ole. He would have killed me. He was crazy with fear. He wouldn't have stopped if I'd only wounded him."

The old man sobbed into his gnarled hands. "*Ya*, I know. All times he was bad boy, dot Ole. But always I had hope he would change. Und den he became murderer."

Satan's face froze. "*He killed Hank?*"

Big Sven looked up, his surprise showing in his face. "You—you know Hank? You know he is here, *ja?*"

"What?" Satan shouted. "Here—in this house—alive?"

Big Sven's face was ashamed. "In der cellar, he bane. He come look for me, ask me question. I bane frightened, because I t'ink he know about Ole. I tell him 'Vait!' und I get Ole, question him. Ole, he go to saloon, talk vit Hank. Und den—" The big railroad man faltered, his head dropping again.

"And then! Come on, man, speak up!"

"Und den he beat up Hank, take him here und put him in cellar, vit' gag und ropes to hold him quiet. Ole say he make him talk, by yiminy, or he kill him. He beat him time and again."

"But Hank wouldn't talk!" Satan's eyes were ablaze. "Doc—and you, Pat, and Solly—go into the cellar and get Hank—if he's still alive. But go carefully. Don't take any chances on a trap!"

The girl was fighting bravely to keep her chin up. But it was plain that she'd had a terrific shock, was humiliated as well. Satan turned, his eyes seeking out The Dutchman.

"Take Sonya downstairs," Satan said. "Fix her up some strong coffee, Dutchman, and see if you can quiet her down. She's had a bad shock. Also"—Satan smiled fleetingly—"see if you can make her understand that we're not a flock of bandits. I have an idea you can put it over, Dutchman."

The jolly-faced fellow beamed. Sonya whispered a tragic "Thank you" to Satan.

The crew leader looked around him curiously, saw only the ordinary furnishings that a hard working, sober man would provide for himself. But he wondered at the size of the house. He questioned Big Sven on it.

"Der vas roomers," the railroad man explained. "I had maid to vork house, to make a home for Sonya ven she is in from her trips. All time since her mother, my second vife, die, I have it so. But Ole, he meet up vit' a gang and he make der roomers get out so his friends can come here."

Satan's eyes were keen. "I see. The gang met here, eh?" He wondered about the dead man, looked at him again. "Your—first wife, Sven. She's dead, too?"

The man nodded his head. "*Ya.* But she vas bad, too, like Ole. She leave me ven Ole vas a baby, ran away vit' a doctor fellow, a Russian."

A light flashed in Satan's brain. "A Russian! And his name was—Vasili Vashter!"

"*Ah!*" A long sigh escaped the big chap. He looked at Satan in awe. "How is it you know everyt'ing?" he whispered. "I nefer see you before, but you know all dese t'ings! *Ya,* Vashter vas der man. He call on me about accident ven I bane hurt, und my vife leave me a week later." He sighed, shook his head. "But der mother of Sonya, she vas good woman. Like Sonya."

Satan turned at the sound of steps on the stairs. Doc, Pat and

Solly entered the room, carrying Hank. The ex-railroad man's face was bruised and swollen, his nose smashed, his lips split. But the game fellow managed a hideous grimace for a smile.

"Cap'n," he whispered thickly, "I—I'm sorry I—bungled things. Ole—Ole kept beating me to—to make me talk."

Satan's eyes were narrowed. "And—did you?"

The injured man shook his head. "No—Cap'n. I didn't. I'd die first!"

Satan turned to Slim. "Three thousand dollar bonus for Hank, when we finish up." He smiled tightly. "Unless we *get* finished up ourselves!" He sobered quickly, turned to Sven.

"Get this straight," he said. "You're in a bad spot, Sven. If you talk now, and talk freely, without holding anything back, I may be able to get you out of it. If you don't—!"

"I talk," the big fellow said simply. "Vat you vant to know?"

CHAPTER 10
THE SATAN SYSTEMS

S ATAN SENT all his men from the room with the exception of Slim. "Get down below stairs," he said crisply. "You, Pat—I want you to go to the roof and stand guard there. If the gang uses this house in 'Frisco, they might have been watching. They might try to steal up on us."

He dropped into a chair and asked Slim to sit down. "Now, Sven, what is this all about?"

"Robbery," the man said directly and simply. "Ole, he bane a robber. He vorked a little at der yards. But not often. I helped him once ven der railroad police vas after him. Den he say he write und tell der line unless I do what he say. He tell me dot if der line hear I help robber to escape, dey fire me, und der transport people dey fire Sonya." He stopped.

"How did you help him? With his thieving, I mean?"

"He tell me der number of der train he vant to know about, und I giff him der numbers of der cars, und vere dey go to. Dot's all I do."

Satan pondered. "I see. And the last train you gave him was Number One-Eleven. Right?"

Big Sven stared. "*Ya.* I giff him der numbers of One-Eleven."

"The numbers of each and every car in the string?"

"*Ya.* Und der Lines dot owned der cars, und der freight der train carried."

"And then what?"

"Dot's all."

Satan stared at the man, was convinced that he was telling the truth. He blinked, looked at Slim. "What do you make of it? Why should Ole have wanted numbers and names of the cars, and nothing else?"

"So they could knock the train off?"

Satan made an impatient gesture. "Why do they need numbers to knock a train off? All they need is a system, and the men to swing it."

Slim scratched his head. "I can't figure it."

Satan considered a long moment. "And you don't know what he wanted with those numbers, eh?"

"Oh, *ya*. He telephone der numbers, sometimes, to Denver, to—"

"Spoletti's," Satan supplied drily. "Now we're getting someplace. And what did Spoletti do with them?"

Big Sven was dumbly ignorant. "He yoost send Ole money, den."

"There's something significant here, Slim," Satan said after a moment. "But the key to it escapes me. Until I get it, we're strapped."

Slim nodded. "Then—that means Denver?"

Satan nodded, turned to Sven. "You haven't given anything out to Ole since Number One-Eleven?"

The man flushed, hung his head guiltily. "I—I giff der Silk Train, last night."

"The Silk Train! My God!" Satan came to his feet with a jump. "Slim! Do you realize what that means? The Silk Train— the freight-express that carries more than a million dollars in raw silk to the manufacturing market in the east for delivery!"

"You think they'll grab it off? How? And why? They'd be nabbed with the silk if they tried to sell it!"

"Hell, man!" Satan strode the length of the room, his eyes ablaze. "They don't sell it. They hijack the loads, then threaten the brokers or the manufacturers who own it with destruction of the cargo and *death* unless they kick in ransom money! Get it?"

Slim shrugged. "That's your guess. But—where do they hijack the trains, and how is it that the trains are seen in three or four places at one time?"

Satan's face went dead again. "I—don't know for sure. But it is all part of The Hyena's scheme to fool the authorities before they unloose the silk for the ransom money."

"What would the silk stand to clear them?"

"Maybe a quarter of a million, roughly. Big game, Slim, big game!"

"But you still don't know how they do it. And Ole is dead. So what?"

"So we check and see if the silk train is missing, to-morrow. Then we crash Denver at the right time and collect—break the ring—turn them in to the Feds!"

"And I still say you got to figure out how they knock off the load, Captain."

Satan's face was dark. But he finally nodded agreement. "You're right. Slim. Go down and detail the boys off to hotels while we get some rest tonight and talk this thing over. Then, to-morrow, we'll pull out. But I'll leave Hank here, for a while. He can't move, yet."

"I'll give the men phony names, assign each to a different hotel, start them off in relays," Slim recited. "Orders are to be on tap at their telephones until they get a call from me."

"Right! But—tell The Dutchman I want him to bunk down here. Sven is on vacation, and The Dutchman is to watch him night and day. I think he's all right—but I'm not taking any chances."

A HALF-HOUR later, Satan and Slim walked rapidly to the corner and hailed a taxi. They sped along the poorer section of the city, then turned and made for the center.

Satan sat in a corner, his face dark and his eyes brooding.

After a while, he stirred. "Damn it all, Slim, why can't we figure this thing out? We've—"

He stopped, his hand gripping Slim's elbow like a vise. "Slim! By the Lord Harry, I think I've got something to work with!" He leaned forward, rapped sharply on the window. "Stop here!"

Sonya

The cab slid to a stop and Satan hurried Slim out. When the driver had been handsomely paid, the leader walked his lieutenant back up the broad business street. He nudged him as they passed the display window of a department store. Tracks… toy trains… bridges… tunnels… all were being set in position by the display men of the great merchandise house in an attempt to attract the trade of children and their parents.

A sign in the window read, *Try your hand at running our electric system on a nation-wide scale. The greatest toy railroad in the world, set up on a map of the United States. Fifth Floor. Toy Shop.*

"We're going to accept their invitation," Satan grinned. "I always did have a weakness for toy railroads! Come on!"

At the rear of the great store, Satan paused, looked up and down the street. "Jimmy that door open," he ordered tersely. "And do a neat job! We'll visit that toy department right now!"

Twenty minutes later, two wraiths ghosted up the stairs of the store to the fifth floor. Slim signaled for caution when they came upon the great display of toys. A watchman was standing nearby, his eyes dreamy. They waited until he moved.

"Get him!" Satan whispered. "Truss him and we'll take him with us. We don't want any interruptions!"

Slim's shadow flitted down an aisle to the right of the unsuspecting guardian of the floor. There was a muffled grunt of surprise when the watchman encountered a gaunt, masked man with a businesslike gun in his hand. Satan, masked, ranged up with several skipping ropes he had found nearby. The watchman's hands were tied behind his back and a gag stuffed into his mouth.

On second thought, Satan ripped the man's tie to shreds, stuffed wads of it into his ears. He grinned as Slim pushed the watchman ahead toward the section where the miniature railroad sprawled across a great map of the United States.

RIVERS, TUNNELS, bridges, mountains, cities and towns were built in dwarf scale across the map that was the floor of the railroad. Satan studied the whole arrangement for a while, then said:

"Rig two sets of freight trains from that stack of spares," he motioned to the little cars. "We'll start both trains from this end, which shall be San Francisco."

Slim worked fast, lined up two freight trains on the toy map, and Satan threw the lever that set them in motion. When they reached the Eastern terminus of the tracks, Satan shook his head. "The thing is crazy," he said.

"What's that? What's crazy?" Slim asked, his eyes puzzled.

"Look," Satan explained. "The trains can go only so fast, can't they. They can't be in several states at the same time, can they?"

"But—they are, somehow."

"No." Satan shook his head. "It merely *looks* that way, just *seems* to be what they're doing. It's an illusion."

"But how come the railroad officials haven't figured that out?" Slim wanted to know.

Satan's eyes bored into Slim. He lighted a cigarette, took a long drag on it. "My guess is that they have figured out some part of it," he said, exhaling slowly. "But—" He paused, pin-points of light coming alive in his eyes, "but the ones who are in the know have been intimidated, threatened with personal violence, threatened with the destruction of a trainload of men, maybe."

"Would that stop them?"

"It would; until they had something tangible to go ahead on."

"Haven't they something tangible, Captain? The manufac-turers to whom the freight has been consigned, the train crews themselves, the men who report the identical train at three different places at one time?"

Satan shook his head. "That, Slim, is the mystery of it, the hokus-pokus that has the railroad officials up in the air. It's—it's supernatural, almost. And that's the very thing that is throwing them off the trail, off the scent. It's like a magician on the stage, who diverts the attention of the audience from what his *right* hand is doing by the simple expedient of making some mean-ingless motions with his *left* hand. Get it?"

Slim shook his head. "No, I don't."

"Okay." Satan threw a lever, brought one of the trains back. "We'll figure it out as we go along." Slim put out a hand to adjust a 'tree' that had been toppled over near one of the rail stations, accidentally knocked another over when his sleeve touched it The train that was being switched hack to 'San Francisco' struck it, derailed, fell from the raised stage of the miniature railroad and to the floor, out of sight.

Slim stood suddenly straight at the noise, swung to look at Satan. The crew leader was staring at the edge of that platform— the edge of the platform over which the miniature train had plunged. His eyes were bright, blazing triumphantly.

"What happened?" Slim asked, puzzled. "That noise—?"

"That noise," Satan said tensely, his face turning to Slim's, "was the explosion of The Hyena's hokus-pokus game, Slim!" He raised a hand, pointed at the train that still rested at the Eastern terminal. "Somehow, Slim," he said. "The hijacked trains leave the tracks and disappear, somewhere east of 'Frisco. It could be anyplace, I suppose, but I've got a hunch about this thing."

"What is your hunch?" Slim asked anxiously.

"Tonopah," Satan said softly. "Tonopah—the place the train crews last remember. Tonopah—the gold mining country of a generation ago. That country is honey-combed with abandoned mines. Furthermore it is virtually deserted at the present time." He paused for a moment, then continued:

"My guess is, the train is run into a mine. In some way it is unloaded. Then the cargo is taken East for delivery, after the money has been paid by the people interested."

"Then—wouldn't the tracks show from the railroads? You couldn't run a spur line to an abandoned mine and hope to have it concealed." He shook his head in doubt. "And, wouldn't that little job be *seen* by somebody—? The switching of that train?"

"It's done at night," Satan argued.

"Okay, it's done at night. But the marks would still show up, Captain."

"Let's hope you're right," Satan said grimly. "We're going out to check Tonopah, in the morning—to check the place they last remember!"

Satan started for the stairs, paused near the watchman. He yanked the wadding out of his ears. "There's a sharp edge on that train stand," he said. "Hobble over there and cut your hand ropes loose. It may take you twenty minutes or so, but it'll be worth it At least you won't look like a boob, having them find you trussed up here."

He stopped long enough to peal a fifty-dollar bill from his roll. He stuffed it into one of the man's pockets. "Thanks for the use of your railroad," he grinned. "And if I were you, I'd keep my mouth shut about this. They'd think you were drunk or crazy!"

The man nodded vigorously, but his eyes were still wide with wonder.

CHAPTER 11
THE FLIGHT TO HELL

THE SPECIALLY chartered transport plane roared over Tonopah in the early morning. Satan, at the controls, banked the ship steeply and stared down at the ground. Slim, at his side, rode nervously but alert.

In the ship in back of Satan sat the entire crew, with the exception of Gentleman Dan, The Dutchman and Hank. Gentleman Dan had disappeared into the night to keep his rendezvous with the deadly Hyena; The Dutchman was cheerfully standing guard over Sonya and Big Sven, as well as looking after Hank.

The squat, ugly buildings that had once been the pride of the world's gold mining center wheeled back under the wings of the fleeting plane. Satan's face was calm, but there was disappointment in his eyes. No marks showed on the ground anywhere to indicate that a switch had ever been laid, a spur track run to one of the abandoned mines below.

"What do you think?" he asked Slim.

The lieutenant shrugged. "Bum guess," he said. "That's what I think. It sounded good, but it isn't—" He stopped, gasped, clutched wildly when Satan zoomed the plane up and cut around in a sharp bank.

"Slim! See down there—that streak of white that shows on the ground! It curves away from the main line and heads into the mountain here, just below us. What do you make of it?"

"Snow," Slim guessed. "Hasn't all melted."

"Any reason why it should melt every other place, but stay in a semi-circle under a burning sun? I'm going down to have a look."

Steeply, Satan nosed for the earth, cutting his throttles back. He climbed down the air trail in a snaking glide, his eyes watchful for a landing place near the railroad. He feathered the large plane down gently on a flat patch of sun-baked earth and rolled to a stop.

In two minutes, they were at the faint white marks. Satan knelt and studied the minute specks that glinted on the ground. He wet a finger, picked up several of the bits, tasted them.

"Borax!"

"Borax?" Slim's eyes were puzzled. The rest of the crew watched in puzzled wonder. "Well, what of it?"

"It looked like snow from above, didn't it? Suppose The Hyena's crew laid a spur at night—and in the snow! How would they cover up the marks after the job had been done? With borax! It wouldn't show until the snow melted... and then it could be swept up and carted away."

Slim nodded. "But—why didn't the Feds spot that? Or the railroad detectives? They must have flown over this stuff, too."

"It looked like snow when they saw it, because there was nothing but snow around it at the time."

"Well," Slim pondered, scratching his head. "That's all okay, Captain. But—that shipment to the Hassem people. There wasn't snow then. And from the looks of it, the sand that leads up to the mountainside hasn't been disturbed since Tonopah was in full blast."

"They may have used some other mine," Satan pointed out. "When they were through they may have spread sand to cover their tracks."

"All in one night?" Slim was incredulous. "They hijack a train, lay a spur, pull up the spur, sand the ground down, get the freight and the crew out, and get away again all in the snap of their ringers?" Satan's face was dogged. "Damn it, Slim, I can only call them as I see them. I know it's impossible as you say it is. Yet, The Hyena is doing it. He's doing it and collecting plenty!"

Slim shook his head. "What do we do now, Captain?"

"First, we follow this track and see the place it leads to. We'll worry about the rest of it later. Leave a guard on the plane, and tell him to say we had motor trouble, in case anyone stumbles over the ship. The rest of us will circle around and approach that mountain from the side. I'm sure I'm on to something, Slim, and I don't want to take any chances of ruining the game now."

KAYO WAS selected to stand guard. He grumbled at being left out of it, but he grinned his relief when Slim pointed out that the rest of them had a ten mile walk to make.

They struck out to the left of the track in the sand and walked through the blistering heat for hours. The earth began to get rougher; great boulders loomed higher than their heads.

When the crew had covered about half the distance to the place where the telltale marks ended, Satan paused. "Slim, as we go along, we'll set a man on guard in these rocks. Space them about a mile apart. Tell them to keep under cover... both as regards the ground and the air. Challenges, should anyone come near them, will be the call letters."

While Slim paused to station a man at his post and give the others instructions, Satan walked on. He stepped onto a rock, then jumped down the other side. He stumbled heavily when his foot found a small hole in the rough earth. He picked himself up and started forward, glancing back to see what it was that had thrown him.

He stopped dead in his tracks.

Around that hole were the prints of numerous heel marks. Satan walked back slowly, dropped to his knees and examined the ground carefully. Slim came on him there.

"Something?"

"Heel marks." Satan pointed out a dozen or more.

"Probably some old desert rat trying to dig himself up enough gold to get by."

Satan shook his head. "Those marks were made by *shoes,* not boots." He dug a hand into the earth near the hole, pulled out a small rock. Others, below that one, appeared to be in a peculiar formation that supported themselves in a wide, disc-like structure. Satan quickly removed a few more, then stopped.

He pulled out his flashlight and stuck it into the hole he had made, snapped it alive. His eyes were agate-hard when he turned to Slim. "An iron ladder, Slim—in that hole. Concealed by those rocks!"

But Slim was still skeptical. "Probably left there by some miner, years ago."

"An *iron* ladder?" Satan's eyes were pitying. Slim blinked, let his gaze rove to the mountainside in the near distance.

"Go back, get two of the boys," Satan snapped. "I'll clear enough of this space for us to get in. If I find what I think I'll find we'll have the boys put these rocks back in place and stand guard while we investigate!"

A half-hour later, Pat and Doc watched their chief and Slim climb cautiously down the ladder. It was all of thirty feet to the bottom. Satan nosed his flash around, let its beam trace a path down a low-roofed tunnel that stretched to the left.

Satan smiled tightly and stared up at the men above. "Put the rocks back into place," he called. "Stand guard there... but keep your ears open for us. If this is a blind, that's the only way we can get out again, and we can't lift the rocks from inside here. We'll give our call-letters when we want to get out again."

"Right, Cap'n."

Satan once again shot the beam ahead of him into the tunnel.

Captain Satan

He led the way cautiously. Slim following behind. The ray of the flash picked a path through the jutting rocks that made the tunnel wall. The damp air of the place seemed to strike a shiver up the crew lieutenant's spine. His teeth chattered slightly, bringing Satan's eyes around to him.

"It's cold down here, Captain," Slim said lamely.

"Cold as the grave," Satan agreed somberly. Then: "But nothing's going to stop me from figuring out this riddle, Slim—the riddle of a modern, thirty-foot ladder in an abandoned mine shaft—and of borax marks leading from the main track to the side of the mountain, like a path of unmelted snow that somehow survived the burning sun."

ABOVE GROUND, Pat and Doc replaced the rocks carefully until they had covered over the place where Satan and Slim had disappeared. Pat climbed to his feet, then turned his masked face up to the sun. From far off came the drone of a motor....

But no plane was visible.

Doc wiped his hands carefully. Then, suddenly, he stiffened. "Did you hear something crunch, Pat?" he asked.

The Irishman listened a moment. "Sure, I thought it was a motor I heard."

Doc waited a minute, then walked around and disappeared behind a huge boulder.

Pat whistled a tune, lighted his cigar and puffed on it contentedly. The motor sound had died. But when Doc didn't reappear in three minutes, Pat stared at the big rock, his brows drawn in a frown. "Hey, Doc," he called.

There was no answer. Pat's eyes went wide. But he reassured

himself. "Just went off investigatin' that noise he thought he heard." He sat down and smoked his cigar to the butt. When he threw it away, his eyes had gone suddenly flinty.

"Sure, 'tis a spooky place," he muttered. "An' Doc, now? Where the divil did he git to, that he's been gone so long?" The squat, red-haired member of Satan's crew slid his gun from its holster, then went stealthily to the rock and around it.

He gasped suddenly when he saw that outstretched form on the ground in front of him. He holstered his gun and sprang to the fallen man's side.

It was Doc!

"Are ye hurt, man?" Pat asked anxiously, shaking Doc gently. He stared at the ominous lump that grew on the man's forehead. And he failed to see the shadow that detached itself from a boulder behind him and slid silently forward.

A powerful, swarthy-faced man crept close, lifted a hand high over Pat's head, then brought a bludgeon down in a sickening blow to his skull.

Pat buckled at the knees, then pitched face down across the unconscious Doc.

"Dat does it!" the blackjacker growled. "Cmon, Dude! We got 'em both."

From behind the rock came another figure, a tall, black-eyed individual with a debonaire mustache. "You certainly did it," the newcomer murmured. "Now what do we do, Spike?"

"We drag 'em away an' do 'em in, up dere in de rocks where dey won't be easy to find—an' away from de tunnel entrance." The swarthy one wiped his perspiring face.

98

"Den we go after de mugs dat went in de tunnel! We got 'em trapped perfect, Dude—de Hyena in front of 'em, an' us in back! Captain Satan's number is up in big, black letters a mile high!"

CHAPTER 12
TRAIL OF THE DAMNED

B EFORE SATAN had gone many yards, he saw signs of the tunnel's constant use and of its obviously modern strengthening and reinforcing. He showed this to Slim as they went cautiously along. They mounted to higher levels only to clamber down again further on as the dark passage twisted through the bowels of the earth.

"Steel and cement props there," he said at one juncture. His flash raked the floor, revealed stubs of white, paper cylinders. "Cigarettes." It went further, revealed matches. It stopped on a newspaper. Slim bent over and picked it up.

"The Denver *Leader!*" Satan's lieutenant breathed. He found another. *"And the New York Mercury!* Both papers are of recent date!"

Satan said drily, "Left by some old miner, eh, Slim?"

The lieutenant shook his head. "You win, Captain. We've hit something."

There was a tenseness about the two as they pressed on, running, almost, in their eagerness to reach the end of the tunnel, to see what it was that lay at the far end of the passage.

Satan estimated that they had been walking about ten

minutes when he stopped suddenly and killed the flash. "What's that?" he breathed.

Slim cocked his head, put out his hand to keep contact with his leader. From somewhere nearby came a high, whining buzz. Suddenly, a roaring sound filled the tunnel, followed by a loud, hissing breath, as of some legendary giant. Satan felt the warm blast that followed. Then everything stilled as suddenly as if a tap had been turned off.

"What the devil?" he muttered. He pressed the flash light on again. He studied the tunnel ahead of them, then snapped the ray off. "Keep your hand on my shoulder, Slim. We'll go by easy stages in the dark."

But they covered a hundred yards, making a slight turn to the right. The whining buzz split the air again. Satan pried cautiously ahead with the flash. Slim's eyes followed the ray— and he gasped.

Scarcely thirty feet ahead of them was a solid wall of rock. They were at a dead end....

While far behind them, at the mouth of that tunnel, the rocks were once again carefully removed and a man with a pistol in his hand climbed swiftly, assuredly, down the ladder and went silently in the direction taken by Satan and his lieutenant.

SATAN AND Slim stopped by the wall. The leader directed his flashlight at the ceiling and the sides of the tunnel, then straight at the rock wall that confronted them.

"Funny," he murmured to Slim, his lips close to the man's ear. "We can hear that buzz so clearly. And I distinctly felt a blast of warm air come down the tunnel. You remember? When that awful racket started up?"

Slim nodded. "Maybe—" He went slightly forward, peered at the wall overhead. He saw what appeared to be a crack in the stone over their heads. "I wonder where that leads to, that crack? Maybe that's where the noise is coming from." He leaned his weight against the massive, cragged wall that blocked the tunnel and stretched up, his eyes intent.

Satan's face went rigid with attention as he watched Slim. He rubbed his eyes, looked again. Slim seemed to be leaning away—leaning—leaning. Satan smothered an exclamation of astonishment and grabbed for Slim's shoulder. He dug his fingers into the man's jacket, hard, his fingers biting into Slim's flesh.

Satan gave a frenzied tug, jerked Slim upright again just as he was losing his balance. Slim's eyes were wide with wonder. He looked at Satan, puzzled. "Was I—falling? But *how?* I was leaning against the rock barrier!" He turned, his eyes following Satan's.

The rough, gray rock that blocked further passage was swaying as if in the throes of an earthquake, lapping back and forth in a swaying, pendulum-like movement. Satan put his hand out, passed it quickly over the vertical surface of the rocks.

His laughter was low, self-mocking, when he turned to Slim. "A curtain!" he whispered. "A simple, ordinary stage prop made up to look like a rock wall—*cardboard and paint!*—and it damned near threw us!"

He stepped forward cautiously, snapping off the flash again. He put out his hand and felt for the side of the camouflaged piece. A beam of brilliant light knifed into the darkened tunnel as Satan drew the curtain to one side. Slim came close, and their eyes riveted on the scene that was uncovered.

In a huge, cavernous area that had been dug out of the earth were set a number of smokeless flares that cast an eerie light, in which more than a score of overalled men toiled silently, intently. They worked like ants in front of that curtain. They were shifting loads and carrying them away. Then returning to shift new loads.

More important, in the center of this activity could be seen a score of steel express cars.

Satan saw the gleam of the many rails that crossed and wove through the great place. Then his eyes followed a man who carried an acetylene torch close to one of those cars. The man jammed the flame against the door lock and opened it. When the many cars were forced open, men began taking square bundles out of the cars and placed them on an electric car that drew alongside the freights. When the electric car was full of bales, it made a turn and disappeared into the gloom. Another loading car rolled up to take its place.

"The train trap," Slim breathed in Satan's ear. "They've got the train in here, God knows how, and they're unloading it!"

Satan stood silent in the gloom of the tunnel for a long minute. When he spoke his voice was flat, awed.

"Right, Slim. And, what's more, it isn't just an ordinary train. You saw those small bales the men were loading onto the electric car? Those bales weigh twenty-five pounds each, Slim—and have come here all the way from Japan."

"*What?*"

"That's right, Slim. That's silk they're unloading. In some way, this gang has snatched the famous Silk Train as easily and as cleanly as a master pickpocket would cut a purse loose from its strap!"

THE TWO stood silent for some minutes. Then Slim spoke: "What'll we do? Get the crew and jump them?"

Satan's voice was caustic. "What's the rush? We haven't got the leader yet, Slim. *Nor* have we got his money. When I smash a gang of crooks, I take everything but their shirts. You know that."

"Oh." Slim stopped; but Satan read the doubt in the man's voice.

"You're thinking that I only take money from crooks that comes from other crooks. Right? But I have no feeling against taking money that's been paid by merchants to this gang. If they'd squawked, it might have turned differently. But *these* owners of cargoes, like the Hassem Company, are satisfied to keep their faces shut and let other manufacturers get taken over. They let railroad and G-men get killed. They don't care, as long as they can get their own precious raw materials back and their plants operating again. If they weren't scared stiff of this mad mob, this outrage could not happen!"

Satan peered intently at the activity, then continued: "No, Slim—anybody who plays ball with The Hyena is guilty himself, and deserves to lose money. And with the length of time that these fellows have been operating, it must be considerable money. I'm going to get it if it's humanly possible!"

Slim asked, "Then you'll watch this stuff, see how they work their game and then crack down?"

Satan's voice was grim. "How long do you think we'll be able to stand around this tunnel, Slim? You saw yourself that it is used quite a bit. We don't dare stay here another minute! The plane isn't quite in sight on the spot where the borax tracks disappear, but sooner or later it's going to be seen. Then there'll be hell to pay."

They stood there for a moment, watching the scene before them.

The leader tensed suddenly. His hand went out to grip Slim's arm. The lieutenant stood absolutely silent. The whine of the electric car started up again, then that mysterious roar once again filled the narrow passage. Hot air breathed through the camouflaged curtain from behind which Satan watched.

Satan stepped to the curtain, peered out. A billow of white smoke rose up in the huge cavern. The torch light revealed the sleek, shining sides of a huge locomotive. The freight cars jolted forward a hundred yards, then ground to a stop again. The swarm of men attacked the closed doors that were brought into their working area.

Satan turned back when the noise died. He told Slim to start back to where Pat and The Dutchman waited. "Hurry," he whispered. "I've got a plan laid out to—"

This time Slim halted, freezing into his tracks. The shuffling scrape of stealthy feet came clearly to them. A spark of light flashed in the tunnel beyond the near turn, then died.

"We're trapped," Slim whispered to Satan, his voice calm, steady.

"Right." Satan was silent a moment. Then: "Get to that

turn and flatten your-
self against the wall.
The man may just get
by you. If he does, jump
him and clamp your
hand over his mouth.
We don't want any noise
to get to those men at
the cars. That's damned
important."

"But—what about
Pat and Doc? If they
were standing guard, how did anyone get by them? Maybe it's
one of our own men, Captain?"

"Hell, no!" Satan's voice was low and sharp. "They were told
to stay there, and they'd stay there until Hell froze over unless I
changed the order. Whoever it is, they've got Doc and Pat. But
they probably don't realize we found that entrance."

The shuffling grew louder.

Slim stole forward soundlessly, his hand against the wall to
guide him. Silence fell again, excepting for that steady, muffled
scrape of the feet coming on—coming on—closer and closer—

The sound became louder. Satan realized the man had
rounded the bend. *Shuff, shuff... shuff, shuff,* came the sounds.
Then a gasp, a choking grunt as Slim struck. Satan snapped his
light on and ran swiftly to help his lieutenant.

CHAPTER 13
THE LIVING DEATH

S ATAN'S FLASHLIGHT picked out the two men who struggled on the floor of the tunnel. Slim's long legs were wound around the torso of the intruder, his arms locked across the man's throat, choking off his breath.

Satan clubbed his automatic, stooped to seek an opening to bring it down hard. The eyes of the straggler met Satan's! The eyes were calm, unfrightened. As Satan stared, he saw one eye close in a wink. He saw the finely chiseled nose, the debonair mustache, the good-looking mouth.

"Gentleman Dan!"

Slim worked on with his throttling until Satan's hand grabbed his wrists, forced them off. "Easy, Slim. It's Dan!"

Slim stared uncomprehendingly at first, then sat back on his haunches and gaped. "Dan?" He whipped out his own flash and trained it on the newcomer. Gentleman Dan grinned ruefully and rubbed his throat. He spoke in a moment.

"Slim the Throttler," he chuckled.

Satan cut in, his voice hard. "Why didn't you sing out your call letters?"

Gentleman Dan got to his feet, dusted off his clothes. "I didn't know whether you'd gone through to the underground yard or not. How was I to know? Until Slim jumped me. And then, I couldn't say anything."

"Where are Pat and Doc?" Slim demanded.

"Back yonder at the foot of the ladder. Spike—that's one of

my new buddies—spotted you fellows working up the side of the hill. I was hoping he'd miss you." He shook his head admiringly. "Nice work, Cap'n—finding that tunnel entrance."

"What are the boys doing *in* the tunnel?" Satan asked, ignoring the compliment. "I told them to stay on top where I left them."

"They couldn't help themselves. Spike ganged up on them, and was going to kill them. But I persuaded him to let them live until The Hyena—" he shuddered slightly, his eyes going hard—"until The Hyena could see them and decide if he wanted them for himself. Right now Pat and The Dutchman are trussed up and gagged."

"Is the entrance closed again?" Satan demanded.

Gentleman Dan nodded. "Right, Cap'n. We're safe here for a couple of hours. Then some more of the gang arrives."

"From where?"

"From about twenty miles beyond Tonopah. That's where the plane lands that's bringing them here."

"Good! Then we can talk. First—how did you get by those fellows in Denver? Our own headquarters was jumped shortly after you left, probably from a tip-off by that man who followed you." Briefly, Satan told of the F.B.I. raid, the escape, of Hank's call and his predicament, of the killing of Ole Kerstadt. "We were afraid you had been trailed, Dan, and that they had tipped off the mob in Denver."

Gentleman Dan nodded soberly. "You were right. I was half way to Denver before I got wise to the man who was following me. I guess he would have telephoned to Spoletti to dust me off, only he was afraid something would go wrong. He wanted to be sure, I suppose, so he came along."

"What happened?"

"He tried to knife me behind a hangar at the Denver airport. But I grabbed his knife and shot him through the temple. Then I stuck my gun into his hand. The papers called it suicide."

"And you went on to Spoletti's—knowing they might be waiting?"

"I had my orders from you," Gentleman Dan said simply.

Satan's eyes glinted. "When did you get here, Dan?"

"Last night, Cap'n. In time to be on the welcoming committee for the Silk Train. The Hyena—"he faltered slightly, —"The Hyena thinks I'm hot stuff. He steered me into a fight with one of his own gunners, at Spoletti's. I shot the daylights out of the place."

"Great work, Dan!"

"Yeah." The man's voice went low, his eyes dropped. "Great work or not, Cap'n—for the first time in my life I'm scared green. I want to get out of this, don't want any part of it. I'll go back to New York and wait for some other job. The boys can have my share." He laughed shortly. "That is, any share that you think you can get out of this—this *devil!*"

Slim and Satan stared. Gentleman Dan was one of the coolest hands in the crew. Yet, he was plainly unnerved.

"What devil? Who, Dan?"

"The Hyena," Gentleman Dan said in a hollow voice. "Doctor—Vashter, as he used to be known!"

A long sigh escaped Satan's lips. "So Vashter is The Hyena!

But—what is it that has you so upset, Dan? It isn't like you to lose your nerve."

"It's the 'Living Death,'" Gentleman Dan said slowly, his voice filled with dread. "The Living Death that Vashter spreads among his men!"

"The—Living Death?" Satan echoed.

Gentleman Dan's eyes slid over the leader's shoulders in the direction of the underground railroad yard. "Did you notice how those men walk without uttering a word? How they work like automatons, like robots? That's the living death of The Hyena!"

While Satan listened intently, Dan went on:

"Every one of those men can work for days and nights on end, without tiring. Any one of them can go a week, two weeks without food. They can live for a month on the water that any one of us would drink in a day." He pushed forward, flashed his own pocket light ahead of him. "Follow me. I'll show you something!" he said.

At the camouflaged curtain, Gentleman Dan drew it boldly aside. They went into the great, weird cavern where the workers plodded methodically, ceaselessly. He stooped to the floor and picked up a stone. Slim gasped when Dan hurled it and struck a man in the small of the back. But the workman never stopped. He never even turned. He dumped his bale methodically, then went to fetch another.

"They're all like that," Gentleman Dan whispered in awe. "No feeling, no sense, no anything but the orders that The Hyena has given them. On and on and on, they work. Day and night, week after week. And they'll go on like that—for the rest of their lives.

Slim had slipped quietly
into the barroom.

That's the Living Death! I don't mind telling you, Cap'n, that it's got me scared. I don't want that for myself."

Satan and Slim watched, the robots work on. It was hard to believe what they saw. Gentleman Dan explained.

"Vashter is a great doctor who went crooked years ago." He

laughed harshly. "It's too bad he didn't stay straight, for he'd have been one of the greatest brain surgeons of all time. He learned his trick operating on a crooked gambler who is supposed to have died twenty years ago—a man that Vashter uses as a ransom collector—Jake Largo."

Satan said, "Then Largo *is* alive! Soapy and Pat were right after all!"

Gentleman Dan nodded. "Vashter cut into Largo's brain, that time of the shooting. He extracted the bullets, and Largo's mob planted a dummy corpse in the casket. When Largo recovered, Vashter discovered that the man could go for days without tiring. He also discovered that he could make Largo do anything he told him."

"Because of the operation?"

"Yes, Cap'n. In taking out the bullets, Vashter took away a neat portion of Largo's brain. Then he reasoned the strange thing out. He snatched a workman off the streets and repeated the operation. It worked. He tried it again—and it still worked. Every one of those men you see in there has half a brain. He can hear, and see, and move. But he doesn't tire, and nothing has any meaning unless it is something Vashter has ordered them to do."

"Great God!" Satan breathed. "But—his nickname, 'The Hyena.' Where does he get that?"

"Vashter didn't do the entire job on Largo that he's done on these others," Gentleman Dan said. "Largo doesn't tire, but he's shrewd, daring and ruthless. He can think for himself. But he's under the domination of Vashter. At first, he rebelled. He tried to break the grip that Vashter was getting on him.

"They shot it out one day—Vashter and Largo—Vashter using his hypnotic powers, and Largo his automatic. Largo ripped the entire upper lip off Vashter's face with his slugs. He shattered his nose and the shot took away part of his jawbone. His own mother would run from him now." Dan shuddered. "He looks like nothing in the world but a perpetually grinning, human hyena."

Satan considered a moment. "Where did you get all this, Dan?"

"Part from Spike. Part from Vashter, himself. But what I know and wasn't told is that sooner or later Vashter will perform that brain operation on every man working with him."

Satan said, "Maybe he will," with primness. Then: "You saw the Silk Train brought in last night?"

"Yes, Cap'n. Neatest thing I ever saw." He parted the curtain from the wall, stepped into the great yard. "Come in and I'll show you how they do it. Nothing to be afraid of in here. These robots won't even see you."

SATAN AND Slim stepped reluctantly after Gentleman Dan. "Vashter's in Denver, eh?" Satan asked.

"Oh, no," Gentleman Dan said coolly. "He's above us on the first level. He's built a place that he could live in for a lifetime, for a century, for a thousand years, and he'd never be found."

"But aren't these men guarded?"

"They don't have to be," Dan said. "These poor devils know only one master; they do only what they are told to do. They can't do anything about it."

Gentleman Dan walked calmly out into the open space and

signaled Satan and Slim to follow. He led the way past the silent robots and stopped at the side of a great tractor. A weird-looking

Slim grabbed the man from
behind and tied his hands.

funnel stretched its long neck from one end and a heavy crane rose at the other end of the giant tractor.

"See that contraption, Cap'n? Neatest thing you ever saw. Here's what happens: The Hyena gets the duplicate numbers and car markers of whatever train he is going to jump, and he—"

Satan cut in on him. "He shoots those numbers East and has a fake train, identical to the one he hijacks, made up. But—*how?*"

Gentleman Dan stared, his mouth wide. "You—you *know?* How in the name of—"

"Get on with it," Satan snapped. "How are the cars faked?"

"The Hyena is a clever devil," said Dan, "and his organization is large enough and crooked enough to pull a lot of tricks. He has crooked agents among the railroad workers and has been successful, a few times, at least, in having empty cars marked the same as the freight he has hijacked. Of course, he can't get away with it forever and probably doesn't intend to. This marking of empty cars is simply to confuse the authorities. It also pleases the vanity of The Hyena to be such a clever tomato."

"And," Satan interrupted, "these phony freights are rolled into the yards bearing the numbers of the original cars, and that's where the railroad people find it? Okay, but what about the train crew?"

"Drugged," Gentleman Dan explained. "Vashter has perfected an odorless and tasteless drug that will knock a man's memory haywire, but permit him to walk around, to eat, smoke, drink. The drug is put into the train crew's drinking water supply by a man on this end of the run. The crew is finally brought East without even knowing what's happened to them."

Satan sighed. "Sounds so simple when you hear it. The man is a genius! A genius, I tell you!"

"He's a human devil," Gentleman Dan said grimly. "I'm afraid of him."

Satan's eyes were narrowed. "Get ahead with it, Dan! How are the trains switched in here? How can they run a train across the sand without any marks showing?"

"That goose-neck flat car," Gentleman Dan said. "See the crane at the other end? When they are ready to spring a job, they roll that contraption out. It lays the necessary rails and the switch to the main line. One of The Hyena's men has already replaced the drugged engineer of the train, and he drives it into the underground yards here."

"What happens after that?" Satan demanded.

"Then, Cap'n, the same contraption is used to pick up the tracks. See that gooseneck thing? See those boxes *under* the car? Those boxes are suction chambers. They suck up sand and stones and stuff, then spread it over the ground in an even layer. The robots go along to fix up any imperfections."

Satan snapped his fingers. "The borax!" he said to Slim. "When they pulled a winter job and couldn't imitate snow, they sprayed borax over the ground. It was whitish, and it blended perfectly with the snow all around it! That was it!"

"You got me there, Cap'n," Gentleman Dan said.

"That all you know?"

"Practically," Gentleman Dan said. "It nearly cost me my life getting that much of it. Here's the rest—as soon as the stuff is hijacked, The Hyena contacts Largo. Then Largo calls on the manufacturers or the owners of the cargo. He puts the fear of God in 'em and collects the ransom. Then, the stolen stuff is taken across country on trucks. The owner gets it eventually, but it costs him plenty."

"But the racket can't go on forever," Satan said.

"I know it, Cap'n," Dan told him. "And The Hyena knows it, too. That's why when they collect the Silk Train ransom, the silk will never be returned. Vashter will simply have it destroyed in the furnaces, and with it, all traces of his crimes."

"What furnaces?" Satan demanded. "And what about the cars?"

"Cut to pieces by the robots as they unload. Destroyed in the big blast furnace on a still lower level."

"It's—it's a stroke of genius!" Satan marveled. "The man is incredible, Slim!" He turned back to Dan again. "But—we know that more than one train with the same numbers has been seen. How about that, if the original train is destroyed?"

Gentleman Dan grinned. "The Hyena has a sense of humor—sometimes. He knows the Feds are watching the tracks. Three times, he's had his robots brought to distant places, had them paint up a string during the night, so the Feds will spot the cars and report them. The railroads suspect the truth, of course. But they're tight shut for fear of causing a panic that would wreck the railroads and the country, both."

While Satan stood turning the thing over in his mind, Gentleman Dan spoke. "But that's all over with one last job that is coming in to-night."

"What?"

The man nodded. "The Hyena knows you're after him. He's giving this game up. But he'll find another, after he stays under cover a while. I know that Largo is dickering for the down payment on the silk now. And that's all they're after. Largo is to fly here with the swag and meet The Hyena. They'll pull one last job before they drop out of sight."

"What job is that?"

Gentleman Dan frowned. "I—don't know. They're tight shut on it. But they're running a mob of gunners in from Denver to handle the thing smoothly. I did hear The Hyena say it would be the biggest thing ever pulled in the history of the world. But I—"

Gentleman Dan faltered to a stop at a shout that came from nearby.

"Dude! Dude! Where are you?"

It was a weird, choked voice with a peculiar nasal quality—as if the speaker was talking with his mouth open, never shutting it.

"God! It's—it's The Hyena! Here he comes! He's calling me!"

CHAPTER 14
THE HYENA

SLIM AND Gentleman Dan went for their guns. But Satan stopped them.

"Cut that, you fools! It's easy enough to kill him. What I want is to smash the whole gang, get his lists of gunners and helpers, if he keeps them—*and his swag!*"

A stooped, slouching figure was visible in the half light. Satan caught the flash of a flare on teeth that seemed to grow out of a

119

distorted nose. He had a glimpse of an eye drawn down horribly at one corner. Despite himself, he shivered. But he grabbed Slim and yanked him around behind the tractor.

Stooping low, Satan scudded along. He crossed to where the robots were plodding with the freight—the priceless silk that was to be destroyed in the blower furnace as soon as Largo got the money. He clubbed his gun and smashed one of the robots. The man never even faltered in his stride.

Again and again, Satan clubbed, desperately. A trickle of blood started from the man's scalp; but he never stopped. "He can't feel it," Satan marveled. "Well—this is the only way!"

He tripped the man, bound his feet with his belt, weighted his body with the square packets that the man dropped. Satan straightened up and tripped another robot. "Get the overalls off your man, Slim," he ordered. "The one I dropped first! Jump into them and start carrying bales. I think The Hyena saw us!"

Rapidly, Satan stripped the overalls from the second man. He pushed him under one of the cars and weighted him down with bales. He pulled on the cover-alls and went quickly to the open door of a car. Slim followed at his heels.

A dead-eyed, yellow-skinned man was standing in that car, methodically pushing out bales. His eyes met Satan's. There was no sign of recognition, of question, of anything.

Satan gathered an armful of the small bundles and began to work stiffly and silently like those poor helpless devils. Then Gentleman Dan's voice came to him as he gathered another load….

"Of course there's nobody here! I been right here, haven't I, for the last half-hour?" Dan was arguing.

"But," the strange voice said, "I saw someone move away as I came up!"

"Your eyes just aren't so good," Gentleman Dan said boldly. Satan saw the two men come from behind the tractor. The hideous-faced Hyena stood with his hands clasped behind him, his eyes fixed on the line of plodding robots. He laughed suddenly, horribly.

"Dude," he said, "I'd kill any other man who spoke like that to me. Aren't you afraid of me?"

Gentleman Dan forced an easy laugh. "Why should I be? You wouldn't harm me, would you? I'm in this racket, too."

The Hyena chuckled frighteningly. "No, Dude! No one shall harm you. Not while you have that beautiful head and that great courage of yours!" The Hyena reached for Gentleman Dan's head, passed his hands over it gloatingly.

"Some day," he chuckled again, "some day I shall make you over, Dude—some day when I have a thousand other men of your nerve and marksmanship! Ah, Dude, with a thousand like you, I could take the Treasury of the United States!"

Satan's eyes narrowed. He averted his face. But he listened as he dumped his cargo and went slowly back.

"Oh, for more like you, Dude! And if only I could get that fool Captain Satan in my hands! I could conquer the world with him, Dude—and a thousand like you!" The man's voice went savage. "Satan's a fool, though! How can he stop me? How can any man stop me? I'll get all my enemies, Dude—in time!

Get them all and make them work for me, *for me!*" He laughed frightfully again.

"And you know how I'll do it, Dude!"

Satan forced his feet to plod onward, though he was tempted to kill the mad genius on the spot. Slim followed, a choking sound in his throat. After a few minutes, The Hyena turned away again.

"Keep a close watch, Dude," he chuckled. "A close watch! My masterpiece is only hours from realization. With that stroke, I'll have the money to gather the right men around me, gather them *and alter them* into a unit of terrible, unbreakable men. We'll climb, Dude—you and Largo and I!—climb to heights of power and riches never before dreamed by man."

Still chuckling horribly, The Hyena disappeared into the gloom.

But he called back: "When Largo arrives, Dude, I shall let you know."

SATAN WAITED until he was sure the man had gone. Then he stripped off his overalls and threw them near his captive. Slim divested his.

"We've got to get out of here," Satan snapped to his lieutenant. "Largo has evidently knocked off the first half of the ransom money. And unless I miss my guess, The Hyena keeps his money salted away upstairs."

"Why not go after it now and clear out of here?" Slim begged. His eyes were glassy, his face pale.

Satan shook his head. "Not until we know what this 'masterpiece' he speaks about is. And I want Largo when I get The

Hyena! Largo and all the rest of the Denver crowd."

"Maybe they'll get us instead," Slim said.

"I'll take my chances!" Satan started away. But he turned suddenly, his eyes blazing. He snapped his fingers and stood staring down at the robots who lay where they had been thrown.

Hank

"Drag them out," he said to Slim and Gentleman Dan. "Drag them out and bring them to me!"

The robots started walking again as soon as their feet were untied. Gentleman Dan steered them at Satan, let them go. Satan put out his hands, stopped the men with one strong arm for each of them.

He fixed first one, then the other, with his piercing eyes. "Turn around," he said tensely. "Turn around and around and around. And keep turning!"

The robots tried to push forward, their feet marking time where they stood. Gentleman Dan and Slim watched, wide-eyed. Satan tried again.

"*Turn!*" he said in a low penetrating voice. "Turn around and around. Turn! *Turn!*"

Slim gasped. One of the robots stiffened suddenly, then slowly started to turn. The other followed. Satan watched, narrow-eyed. In a circle they went, around and around. Satan watched, then barked at them: "Stop!"

They stopped. The leader walked close, held out the overalls that he signaled Slim to bring him. "Put these on," he commanded. *"Inside out!"*

Deliberately, without emotion or resentment, the robots turned the overalls inside out and climbed into them.

"Back to your work," Satan said in that low voice again. "Carry bales. Carry—carry—carry."

The robots turned and went back to their tasks. Slim wiped his forehead. "Listen, Captain—don't *you* get that way, too!"

"We've got to work fast," Satan told his men. "You, Dan— turn Pat and Doc loose, then climb out and give your pal Spike a sock over the head. Slim will follow, and take him with you. I'm not leaving any more men here than I have to."

Gentleman Dan had already gone through the curtain of fake stone and was running swiftly down the dark passage.

"Slim!" Satan called. "Tell Kayo to pilot that plane back to 'Frisco and pick up The Dutchman." He stopped, his eyes brightening. "And bring Big Sven! Tell him we've got a man he'd like to see—one Vasili Vashter. I have a hunch that Big Sven may prove useful to us tonight."

"Right, Captain."

"And get the rest of the men we stationed around as guards and hide them among the rocks. I want them to stay out of sight until we tell them to come. And when we do, they're to use the tunnel passageway."

"Right, Captain."

Satan paused to light a cigarette. "I'm curious about this one last job of The Hyena's." He puffed slowly, his eyes steady on Slim. "You start now, Slim—and see that my orders are carried out *exactly!* When Kayo comes back, have him land the plane from a high altitude. Have him cut his motors from very far away. I don't want any motor sounds to get to The Hyena and interfere with his plans in the slightest."

"And—you, Captain?"

"I'm going to scout after The Hyena, locate his hideout on the upper level. I want to be all set to strike fast and hard, and get away with the entire swag!"

Slim was aghast at Satan's proposal; but he turned obediently and went through the camouflaged curtain and out of sight. After a moment, Satan ground his cigarette under foot and walked slowly out into the gloom in which The Hyena had disappeared.

He snapped his flash on, nosed it around until its ray picked out a wall. He moved along the wall and mounted a staircase hewn out of the stone. He followed it. At the foot of the steps, he snapped the flash off and stared up into the darkness. A faint crack of light showed at the top.

Satan mounted cautiously. He stopped a full minute before he stepped to the landing. When he moved again, he saw that a door was open slightly. It threw a dim light into the passage. He put an eye to the crack, and peered in. The room was apparently empty. There was a small, stout safe in one corner. Under a flat-

The girl stepped out of the closet at Satan's command.

topped, bare table was a square, covered box. Against the far wall stood more than a dozen giant water bottles, all of them filled.

Satan stood in utter silence a moment, then pushed the door in front of him. It was of heavy stone, as were the floor and walls of the room he was entering. His gun ready, Satan stepped forward.

The world crashed down on his head a split second later, and darkness enveloped Captain Satan.

The Hyena dropped down lightly from his hiding place and stood chuckling over Satan.

"You kept me waiting a long time, Satan... a *long* time." The hideous man rubbed his hands together gleefully and stooped to pass them over the crown of Satan's skull. "But it's been worth it, Satan!" gloated The Hyena.

SATAN AWOKE with a splitting headache and a strange hum in his ears. He sat for a moment with his eyes shut, collecting his wits.

Then the memory of it flooded back over him. He recalled entering The Hyena's great stone room, then the world crashing down on his head. He made a slight movement, but felt the strain of ropes on his wrists and ankles. Voices spoke: they seemed to be far away. Satan listened through the cloud that held his head.

"...Sure you didn't crack his skull? He's been unconscious for three hours, now."

A jarring cackle sounded—The Hyena's voice: "So much the better if I did. I can fix his skull—*and* brain! You know that, Largo!"

Satan heard the snarl that answered The Hyena. "Largo!" he thought, his mind clicking back into a groove. "Largo is here—

127

with the money! That means he's set for flight as soon as his *last job* is through!" Satan sat silent; he felt the eyes of the two men on him. Largo spoke again.

"It's queer he doesn't move." Satan wondered at the flat, dead voice of the man who had lost his soul to The Hyena.

"Satan's been working night and day to get me," The Hyena said. "Remember, Largo, he isn't like you… *yet*. Satan still tires, like any other normal man." The Hyena gave his throaty chuckle. "But after I operate, Satan will be like a dynamo, like a tireless machine. *And bent to my will as you are!*"

Satan sensed the struggle that Largo was making, must always be making, against this man, his master. Defeat was in the man's voice when he spoke after a long silence. "Yes— Vashter. Yes! It is your will."

"Good!" The Hyena couldn't quite hide the relief in his voice. "Now we shall talk business: First, you have brought the silk freight ransom with you—a hundred and fifty thousand dollars. That was a good deal you made there, Largo. A pity we can't risk collecting the other half."

"Why don't you? Satan is in your hands now."

"Ah! But not his men! And after we make the *Red Comet* vanish, we do not dare operate again in this same way. No, Largo—I shall content myself with the *Red Comet* and perhaps a hundred of the nation's most celebrated people to hold for ransom. A million dollars is little money for that catch, Largo!"

Satan's brain was awhirl. "The *Red Comet!* The country's crack trans-continental train… New York-bound with scores of movie stars, great industrialists, statesmen, bankers, professional men! God, he can't do it! The man is insane!"

But his common sense told him that not only could The Hyena do it… *he would!* He forced the loud hammering of the blood to still in his ears. The two were speaking again….

"What if you don't get the ransom? What if the chase gets too hot?" Largo inquired.

The Hyena laughed. "My dear Largo! If I do not get the million, I operate on these brains, these brilliants that I am getting in my net. I operate and bring these intellects under my domination. Imagine—I, Vasili Vashter, the absolute master of a hundred, perhaps *two* hundred, of the best minds, the rarest beauty and the finest culture in America! And with Captain Satan at their head!" the madman concluded.

A sudden clamor came filtering through the stone door of the place. Satan wondered. But The Hyena spoke on.

"Six hundred thousand dollars I have in this room, now," he whispered. "More than half a million. And under this desk enough dynamite to blow this very mountain to the skies, should anything go wrong. Blow the place to bits and hide forever all trace of the *Red Comet* and its gay brilliant cargo. And make my escape with my fortune." His voice dropped to a whisper again. *"My fortune—and you and Satan and The Dude, to start anew!"*

After a silence in which the uproar below increased, Largo asked: "Everything is ready? The—drug?"

"In those bottles against the walls," The Hyena said. "But the *Red Comet* passengers have already had enough to keep them

129

powerless and thoughtless for many an hour. There is but one change in my plan, Largo."

"And that is?"

"The crew and all the passengers, excepting the ones I select for ransom—*or* my future assistants—must die. It is too risky otherwise. The robots have been provided with knives." He chuckled madly again. "Largo—my robots will even kill themselves and burn their own bodies… down to one last man! I can do with them as I please."

Largo asked, "That noise in the lower level. What is it?"

"My men are here from Denver. The others are getting the tractor and the rails ready to meet the *Red Comet* in two hours, Largo. We must hurry. Even with our speedy system, we must hurry. We have no time to spare!"

Satan heard the men get up. The Hyena commanded. "Go below! Bring one of my robots. He shall stand guard over Satan, in case he awakes before we return."

Satan's blood curdled when Largo left. The Hyena came over and fondly ran his hands over his head. He felt the sharp line with which The Hyena drew a fingernail across his skull, tracing the spot where his knife would enter. "Here, I shall cut! And here—and here!" the madman chuckled.

Then Largo was back. A shuffling thing walked before him. Satan heard The Hyena's growl of displeasure. "Fool! Why did you not let him drop the bales before he came up?"

Largo did not answer.

The Hyena spoke slowly and emphatically to the robot and

pointed to Satan. "You watch this man. Kill if he moves! You watch man. Kill if he moves!"

Satan heard the bales crash to the floor. He heard Largo's and The Hyena's steps as they went out the door and down stairs. Slowly, he opened his eyes.

In front of him stood a robot with knife in hand. The large, flat, dead eyes were fixed unblinkingly on Satan.

Satan looked back at the man steadily. Then his eyes dropped—and he started. The robot raised the knife in a threatening gesture. But Satan didn't notice. He was seeing those overalls that the man wore—overalls that were turned inside out. This was one of the robots he had commanded in that lower level!

CHAPTER 15
HUMAN FREIGHT

SATAN SAT in silence for a long minute. Then, drawing a deep breath, he ordered: "Use—knife; cut—ropes. Use knife—cut ropes."

Slowly, the robot raised the knife over his head. He came close, brought the blade in a sharp, downward arc. Satan never flinched. *"Cut—ropes!"* he barked.

The robot blinked, swerved the knife and slashed down between Satan's ankles. The leader checked his sigh of relief, then pinned the robot with a steely stare. "Cut—ropes—on—wrist. Cut—ropes—"

The robot moved slowly and mechanically around the chair.

131

There was a hissing swish and Satan's hands went free. But he held steadfastly to his chair. "Put—knife—on table!"

The robot moved obediently and set the blade down. "Stand—still!" Satan ordered. He got to his feet warily, then snapped the knife from the table and dropped it into a pocket. The robot stood still as stone. When he was satisfied that the man had gone into a trance and would stay there until commanded to move again, Satan stared around him.

Against the wall, near the great bottles of 'elixir'—The Hyena's drug to kill memory—was a small, flat, leather case. Satan crossed to it quickly and snapped it open. It was filled with neat stacks of currency. Satan glanced at the safe. Half-heartedly, he tried the handle. He was surprised when the thing swung lightly in his hand.

"Why not?" he reasoned. "How is anyone to get a suitcase out of here? Or anything else with money in it?"

His eyes were visibly impressed by the great tiers of bills that were stacked to the top of the small safe. "Denominations can't be very large," he saw. "The Hyena is smart there!"

He turned to stare at the robot; his eyes dropped to the floor. At the robot's feet were a half-dozen small bales. Satan's eyes narrowed as he looked. Then, moving with lightning speed, he grabbed up one of the silk-weighted squares and stripped the cloth covering away. He dumped the silk onto a table, then crossed to the leather case. Into the leather case he stuffed silk, and into the bales he stuffed the money.

Satan worked with feverish haste, and filled three more bales from the safe. When he had emptied the small vault, he thrust the leather case and the remainder of the opened silk into it and slammed the door shut. With fast fingers, he twirled the combination shut.

"Un—dress!" he snapped at the robot. Even as the robot moved, Satan stripped off his suit and passed it to the man, ordered him to put it on. He snatched up the cut ropes from the floor and tied the robot securely into the chair.

"Stay!" he commanded.

He climbed into the man's overalls and picked up the bales. Then he started cautiously down the stone steps for the lower level. He stopped in the gloom of the lower landing and stared at the figures darting about in the light of the flares.

The Hyena was directing the backing of the remaining cars of the Silk Train, cutting them into a side track to make way for the *Red Comet*. The tractor was gone, and the pile of rails was missing from the side wall. Robots paraded stiffly around, hauling, carrying, shifting.

Satan stood rigid, his eyes studying the setting. Against the far wall it was dark, and to those men standing amid the flares, that wall would seem darker still.

Holding the bales rigidly in front of him, and walking stiffly, Satan made his way slowly to that dark side. He slipped along to the front of the underground. His eyes were keened for that curtained section. But it was so cleverly conceived that he almost missed it.

Without faltering in his stride, Satan lurched against the curtain and plunged into the darkened outer passage.

Without a light, working from memory alone and hardly

knowing when he would crash down to one of the many lower levels in the long tunnel, Satan sped through the utter dark. He smashed into walls at turns. Twice he barked his shins as he fell up some steps. It seemed an interminable distance.

But at last he felt the rungs of the ladder bite into his arms. He raised his head, still clutching the bales tightly. "It's Captain Satan!" he called. "Open up! It's Captain Satan!"

After a moment that seemed an age, he heard the rocks of the entrance being pulled loose, felt the dark, cool air of the night as it rushed in on him.

A light flashed in his face. Men swarmed down the iron ladder to give him a hand. Satan clutched five bales to him, though, as he mounted.

Slim stared. "You O.K., Captain?"

Satan snapped, "These five bales have more than half a million dollars in them. Guard them closely!" He slid them to Slim. "The boys get here, on their return trip?"

"An hour ago. There's hell to pay up the tracks, Captain. Tractors, cars, gunners—" The leader interrupted quickly.

"They're snatching the *Red Comet*," Satan told them quietly. "I've got no time to stand here and tell you all I know. Take orders, all of you—and work fast! Ready?"

"Shoot!"

"Sneak up on track crew that's moving tracks, but don't jump until *after* the *Red Comet* has started in. At all costs stop that tractor from following the train! The gunmen will probably ride the train into the underground. Let them! And then stop that tractor! That'll get all the gang back into the underground—where I want them!"

"How many men for the tractor job, Cap'n?"

The knife was raised, about to strike.

"Two. Is Big Sven here?"

"Bane here, Satan," the big fellow answered simply.

"Good. Doc and Pat—you take the tractor job. You owe those mugs a return engagement. The rest of you follow me, with the exception of Kayo. Where is he?"

"Here, Captain."

Satan squinted into the dark at the man. "Where's your plane?"

"Around the other side of the bend, Cap'n. I dropped her neat!"

"Nice work, Kayo. You get the dough in these bales into the plane. Set your ship for a fast take-off. And guard it with your life."

"Right, Cap'n."

"The rest of you follow me and listen carefully as we go. I'm supposed to be The Hyena's prisoner right now, and I've got to get back to my cell before he finds out there's anything wrong."

"Why don't we blow now, Cap'n?" Gentleman Dan asked. "We got the dough. We can contact the *Red Comet*, and stop it before it gets here."

"Can't. The train crew and all the passengers are doped by now. Besides, even if we did stop it, which we couldn't without bloodshed, The Hyena and his gang would be at large."

It was a grim crew that paced back down the long tunnel with Satan at their head. Near the curtain, the crew leader stopped, took over the bales that he had carried out along with the money bales. He stepped stiffly through the camouflage curtain and walked slowly down the darkened side.

136

At the stairs he turned, walked slowly up. The robot was still seated as Satan had left him.

Two minutes later, the robot was standing before Satan, the knife raised threateningly. And the leader was sitting quietly in the chair, with faked bonds on his wrists and ankles.

IT SEEMED ages to Satan before a roaring gulf of sound filled the underground. He stood then, dropping the ropes. He ordered the robot, "You—follow—me. If—man—touch—*you kill!*"

Obediently, the thing tracked him down the steps, stopped when Satan stopped. The crew leader gasped at the sight that met his eyes.

A great, streamlined, dark maroon locomotive was nosing slowly into the underground, its nickel furbishings gleaming proudly in the light of the flares. Behind it rolled more than a half-score of maroon-red sleeping coaches.

Satan blinked when the lights of the cars gleamed through the glow of the flares. Despite the late hour, every light was on, every shade up, just as they had been, Satan knew, when The Hyena's memory-killing drug had struck them senseless.

Silhouetted in the windows, heads erect but eyes blankly straight in front of them, were the passengers of the *Red Comet,* the very cream of American business, professional and social life.

"Human freight… and cattle for the slaughter… every last one of them!" Satan breathed.

His eyes went narrow at the figures hanging from the platforms of the train— hard-faced gunmen who stared silently at the hunched hideous leader whose warped brain had conceived this.

But The Hyena had reckoned without the steel heaps that lay near the end of the underground cavern—the Silk Train cars that had been cut by torches that very day, but the wreck of which had not been taken to the blast furnace for destruction.

The locomotive puffed to a halt. The Hyena screamed curses and ran swiftly to the side of the cab. He yelled up at the gunman engineer who had taken over the throttle. The regular engineer and his assistant stood staring stupidly ahead at nothing at all.

The Hyena's engineer pointed at the debris and shrugged. The Hyena stared, then motioned to the men in the vestibules.

"Get down," he shouted. "Get down, all of you! We'll have to clear this mess away before we can shut the underground gate on the train!"

The gunners dropped down. Satan sucked in his breath at this unforeseen development. But his eyes whipped to the left as a shadow dusted along behind The Hyena, then hastened through the gloom for the stairs.

Satan stepped away fast. He turned at the other side of the locomotive to watch. Largo hove into view, rapidly, stooping low, and went swiftly up the stone steps!

Satan blinked. This was something unexpected. But he drew his flash and signaled with it quickly toward the curtain at the far end. The Hyena was on the opposite side issuing orders. He couldn't see Satan or the robot where they stood.

Satan's face tightened when he saw his men steal out from that stone camouflage and come down the line of cars, hugging close. Madly, he waved them back. "Back! Back!" he signaled with his light. He wanted them to stand guard at the mouth of the tunnel to block the escape of any of the gangsters.

But he knew his men didn't understand what was happening or how it would alter his plans. He was running toward them when a frenzied scream split the air, bringing silence to all other sounds.

It was Largo—coming down the stairs, his face crazed and a stick of dynamite in his hand! Satan gasped. But Largo was shouting something....

"You thieving devil! You've taken the money, you've taken the money!"

The Hyena stood still a split second, then added his own crazed howls to those of Largo. "Liar! You half-brained rat! What are you trying to put over on me!"

Largo trembled violently. "It's a frame-up!" he screamed again. "You've taken the money and you've hidden Satan and that robot guard to make it look as if *he* took it—as if Satan could get loose and take the money!"

An animal cry sounded in the underground and The Hyena broke into a run. He slammed past Largo, knocking the man to one side. Largo tripped, fell with the stick of dynamite. Satan choked with horror.

But it didn't go off.

Largo left it on the ground and chased up the steps after The Hyena.

Satan thought fast. "Largo thought he saw a chance to sneak

the dough and make a getaway! He thinks The Hyena copped the booty—and The Hyena thinks that Largo got it!"

He snapped around. "Fetch—dynamite!" he told the robot. "On—floor—near—stairs."

The robot walked slowly to the deadly stick and picked it up. He brought it back to Satan, and then a voice spoke.

"So it's *you!*"

Satan swung. The door on the off-side of one of the sleeping coaches had been opened. A man stood at his side, now—eyes burning into him.

It was Jo Desher, head of the Criminal Bureau of Investigation!

CHAPTER 16
DEATH CHARGES DOUBLE

SATAN WAS ice-cool. He smiled faintly and dropped his eyes to the flat automatic that Desher was training squarely on the pit of his stomach. "Don't let that go off," he said calmly. "Or this stick of dynamite I'm holding will pop and take you and me and the *Red Comet* and all its passengers to Kingdom Come!"

Desher blinked. And while he stared, the robot came slowly forward and grappled with him. The F.B.I. chief cursed in a blind rage. Slim and Big Sven and the others came on the run. Satan tripped the robot, ordered Slim to tie him.

But the man had succeeded in disarming Desher.

Satan's crew, masked, surrounded the Federal man. "You

damned fool," Satan murmured, his eyes grim. "I ought to kill you! Did you come on that train by yourself?"

Desher glowered. "We got a mysterious tip-off on the Silk Train. I flew out to check on it, but there was nothing to it. I was taking the train back."

Satan smiled and shook his head pityingly. "Nothing to the story of the Silk Train, eh, Desher?" He nodded at the wrecked trains piled at the far end. "What do you think that junk is— chewing gum?" He pointed a hand at the bales strewn about the place. "Is that silk or isn't it?"

Desher gaped. But Satan inquired gently, "Did you drink any water while you were on the train—Jo?"

Dumbly, the F.B.I. man shook his head. Plainly, he wanted to ask questions, but was too proud to. "No, I didn't," he snapped.

"My, my!" Satan said. "You simply must have a drink, Jo." He motioned to Slim. "Get him a drink of water. Slim—from the train supply. But go carefully. Don't let those gunners on the other side there see you!"

Desher snapped, "You can't make me drink that water." He frowned. Then: "What's the matter with the stuff?"

Satan didn't answer. But when Slim came he gripped Desher's arm and hauled him close. With an iron hand, Satan forced the F.B.I. chief's mouth open, slammed some of the liquid into his mouth. He clapped his hand over Desher's nose and mouth until the man had to breathe—and swallowed first.

"Gentleman Dan? Did you say this stuff made you forget everything up to two hours before?" Satan asked.

"Right, Cap'n."

Satan smiled slightly. "Two more shots of that stuff, Slim. Let's play safe! We don't want this guy to know us too well."

And Desher got the required dose.

Satan saw the Government operative's eyes go dull, his muscles relax. He turned, picked out Big Sven. "You have a lot coming to you, Sven. How'd you like to pilot the *Red Comet* into Salt Lake City and report to the railroad authorities that you found the train stopped, and all the crew and passengers doped?"

"By yiminy!"

Satan flashed a signal to Gentleman Dan. "Get up to the cab there with Big Sven. Shoot the hell out of anyone who tries to stop you. Sven will back the train out of here. You, Slim—take two men and cover the underground exit. As you start, the rest of us will jump The Hyena's gunners. When we get them under control, I'll herd the robots into the tunnel and station them there under orders not to move. Then I'll *personally* go after Largo and The Hyena. Desher might like to have them as a present when he wakes up!"

Satan's men were jumping to their posts when a maddened scream sounded from the stairs again. "Drop that dynamite! Drop it, I tell you, Largo! *Drop it!*"

The gunmen on the other side of the train broke into panicky chatter. Satan heard. "Fast!" he ordered.

Big Sven swarmed up the side of the cab in the wake of Gentleman Dan. There was a brief scuffle, then the roar of an automatic. Sven's hand dropped to the throttle and the locomotive's brakes loosed with a hiss of air.

There was a rush of feet on the other side, followed by a few shots. Satan's men were at the underground entrance, stopping the flight of the gunmen. A fusillade broke a thousand echoes from the walls and the low roof.

With the pitched battle in progress, Satan dropped the stick of dynamite into his pocket and came quickly around to the other side of the train. The robots were standing in a group, their eyes dull, their faces blank.

"Tunnel," Satan clipped at them tersely. "Tunnel—and stay—until—I—call."

The Men of the Living Death broke into movement and walked stiffly around the locomotive. They marched unhurriedly for the curtain with Satan leading them. The locomotive was in motion when Satan saw the last of the robots disappear behind that curtain.

The shots were dying. Fitfully, automatics barked as Satan's crew mopped up the gangsters. Satan signaled to Big Sven when the train had cleared the entrance. The *Red Comet* slowed to a stop.

In the underground, the gangsters lay on the floor, some motionless, others writhing in agony. But Satan was pitiless, ruthless, where these arch enemies of the Law were concerned. His first duty was to get the *Red Comet* clear, then to get Largo and The Hyena.

Slim came on the run. "How many of our boys?" Satan asked in a hard voice.

"The Dutchman and Solly were nicked. That's all. The rest are perfectly okay."

"Good! Hold the train while I get those two devils in the upper level. Get the boys on board. We'll—"

Satan stopped, his eyes going wide. There was a crashing of shots from inside—but far away. "My God! Get the train going! Quick! Those madmen must have been opening the safe. They found it empty and are staging a gun fight!"

"But, Captain, you—"

"Back the train, damn it! There's a box of dynamite in that room! If it goes—!"

Satan and Slim swarmed into the locomotive as Sven slammed the train back at full speed. From somewhere a rumble started that rose over the noise of the engine—a rumble that grew louder, and sent orange flame down the stairs of that underground cavern.

The earth shook with the full throated roar that followed. A blaze of light like the yawning of Hell itself grew in front of the train. It blinded the men in the locomotive cab. When they could see again, the headlight of the *Red Comet* shone on the blank face of the mountainside.

"Gone!" Slim breathed. "Swallowed up as surely as if it'd never been there! And—those poor devils of robots in that tunnel!"

"They're better off there," Satan said in a low voice. "The Men of the Living Death have gone to the only peace they'd ever know."

SATAN STOOD and watched the *Red Comet* slide back on the main track again. Pat and Doc were at the rear, setting red flares as a precaution should another train come along.

When the train was backed sufficiently, Soapy and Slim jock-

144

eyed the tractor into place and yanked the switch clear. Satan watched them trundle it away, drop it a quarter of a mile from the tracks. He turned to The Dutchman.

"Think you could run that tractor? You and Solly?"

The big man nodded and Satan continued: "We won't have time to lift the rails and drag them back to that mountain. And anyway, we couldn't get them in. The landslide has blotted out all semblance of an entrance there. Just spray sand and dirt over the rails all the way back to the mountainside, then drive the tractor out again and abandon it near Tonopah."

"And then, Cap'n?"

Satan stretched. "We'll be gone by then," he said. "Have you got enough money to get back to San Francisco?"

"Have I!" The picture of Sonya Kerstadt was large in The Dutchman's face.

"All right," Satan snapped. "Do that. Take the plane back when you're ready. Or when Miss Kerstadt is flying back. It amounts to the same thing. Slim will contact you and arrange to pay your shares in three days. Be at your telephones then—or you may miss the pay-off."

"Oi," Solly said, "I'm practically at it now!"

Satan called up to Big Sven, "We'll grab a lift down the line, a bit nearer Kayo and the plane. Open her up, Sven!"

When Satan signaled for Sven to slow down again, he gave him some advice:

"Sven—forget you ever saw me or heard of me. Forget that place back there—the railroad that has disappeared! The roads and the government would have to lift that mountain to prove your story. And then you'd only get into trouble. Just tell them you went to Tonopah while on vacation and woke up with the roar of an earthquake in your ears. You investigated to find the *Red Comet* at a dead stop, with all the passengers and crew doped. They'll check that water—and they'll find the burned fuses. And you'll get something more than a dispatcher's job out of the thing!" Satan added.

Big Sven's face glowed.

"Und… dot devil Vashter iss dead!" he whispered.

IN THE plane as it roared eastward, Satan turned to Slim.

"Kayo pilots pretty well, doesn't he?"

"He better keep right on piloting, too. When the gang that rented us that ship catches up with us—"

"Nonsense," Satan said calmly. "I'll buy it for Kayo as a bonus. He earned it. He wasn't in on any of the fun."

"That's a bet, Cap'n," Kayo yelped happily.

"Slim," Satan said after a pause. "I want to drop Desher a letter as we go over Salt Lake City. The poor devil won't know what it's all about, when he wakes up—probably won't even know about the Silk Train."

"How'll we address it?" the tall man asked.

"To Jo Desher, Chief, Federal Bureau of Investigation, Aboard The Eastbound *Red Comet*—Dear Jo: Let me be the first to congratulate you on the breaking of the Phantom Cargo gang. And let me be the first to tell you what part you played in it—because you don't remember—"

Satan broke off, his eyes stormy. "Slim! Write with your *left* hand! Let's start all over again. *To Jo Desher, Chief of the F.B.I. Dear Jo: Let me be the first—"*

WHEN THE Indian Museum closed its doors the next night in New York, two shadows crept from a hiding place and started a methodical collection of the objects that the Museum proudly displayed to an indifferent public. There were knives with carved handles, fire-makers, tomahawks, moccasins, beaded headbands, scrolled leather sheaths and other relics of a vanishing people. These strange articles left the building in the possession of the shadowy figures.

The spooks ghosted down the wide stairs and slid out onto Riverside Drive. A swift, black car eased around the corner and a door popped open. The Indian collectors climbed in and shut the door quietly.

CHAPTER 17
THE LIFE OF RILEY

CARY ADAIR raised politely inquiring eyebrows when a hammering thumped loudly through his penthouse apartment.

Jeremy came quietly from the service pantry, a frown on his face. He snapped the door open, gave voice to a cold "How do you do, Mr. Desher."

The F.B.I. chief walked slowly into the big living room, his eyes cloudy. "Lo, Cary," he said gruffly.

"Nice to see you, Jo. Care for a drink?"

"No."

"Cup of coffee?"

"No."

"Glass of—water?"

Desher's eyes batted and his brows contracted. "Water," he muttered. "Water?"

Adair smothered a smile and looked at Jeremy. "Yes—water! I don't suppose you ever heard of the stuff. Jeremy! Bring two highballs."

"Yes, Mr. Adair."

Desher sat in a moody silence for some minutes. Then: "Cary? I've been on a little trip." When Adair sat in silence, he added, "Remember that—*Phantom Cargo* gang you spoke about before I left you?"

Adair frowned. "I don't get you, Jo."

"Remember," Desher went on—"I told you about the disappearing freight, and you called it *phantom cargoes?*"

"Did I?" Adair sipped his drink. "Clever of me, wasn't it? Did I tell you, Jo, that instead of taking a trip to collect Indian *objets d'art,* that I saved myself the trouble and bought a few? Jeremy— bring our pieces for Mr. Desher to look at!"

"Listen now, Cary—" the Federal man began, "I haven't time to—" He reached his hand for a drink, blinked when Jeremy walked slowly in with it on his tray.

"I'm—losing my memory lately," Desher mumbled as he guzzled the thing. He looked with distaste at the tomahawks and various other relics which Jeremy laid out for his inspection. "Hm."

Adair whirled his glass and made a musical sound with the ice tinkling against the crystal. "Now, about this Phantom Cartoon business, old man. You were saying—?"

"*Phantom Cargo!*" Desher growled. He shook his head sadly. "My God, Cary—why is it you're so dumb at times!"

Adair sat straight. "Now, really, Jo!"

"Oh, hell, I'm sorry, Cary. Only—"

Adair smiled. "I accept your apology. What about this Phantom Cargo thing, old chap? I do recall saying it, now that you press me. Clever, wasn't it?"

Desher grunted. "And it was repeated by another clever man—a *very* clever man, Cary!"

"Interesting, I'm sure," Adair murmured. "Now, this tomahawk, Jo." He looked up suddenly. "Oh! You're not interested, are you? I'm sorry. You'd be surprised at the trouble I went to for them!"

Desher swallowed the last of his drink. "I'll bet! That's all you've got to do—lead the life of Riley and collect Indian tomahawks! Why don't you do something worth while, Cary!"

Adair sat silent for some time after Desher had gone. Then: "Jeremy! Desher is right."

"Yes, sir?"

"Yes! I'm going to do something useful. I'm going to send those curios to the Indian Museum! Make a note of it."

"*Yes,* sir."

Adair drained his drink, signaled for another.

"But make sure you deliver it at night!" he said with a smile.

POPULAR HERO PULPS AVAILABLE NOW:

THE SPIDER
☐ #1: The Spider Strikes — $13.95
☐ #2: The Wheel of Death — $13.95
☐ #3: Wings of the Black Death — $13.95
☐ #4: City of Flaming Shadows — $13.95
☐ #5: Empire of Doom! — $13.95
☐ #6: Citadel of Hell — $13.95
☐ #7: The Serpent of Destruction — $13.95
☐ #8: The Mad Horde — $13.95
☐ #9: Satan's Death Blast — $13.95
☐ #10: The Corpse Cargo — $13.95
☐ #11: Prince of the Red Looters — $13.95
☐ *NEW:* #12: Reign of the Silver Terror — $13.95

OPERATOR 5
☐ #1: The Masked Invasion — $13.95
☐ #2: The Invisible Empire — $13.95
☐ #3: The Yellow Scourge — $13.95
☐ #4: The Melting Death — $13.95
☐ #5: Cavern of the Damned — $13.95
☐ #6: Master of Broken Men — $13.95

THE MYSTERIOUS WU FANG
☐ #1: The Case of the Six Coffins — $12.95
☐ #2: The Case of the Scarlet Feather — $12.95
☐ #3: The Case of the Yellow Mask — $12.95
☐ #4: The Case of the Suicide Tomb — $12.95
☐ #5: The Case of the Green Death — $12.95
☐ #6: The Case of the Black Lotus — $12.95
☐ #7: The Case of the Hidden Scourge — $12.95

G-8 AND HIS BATTLE ACES
☐ #1: The Bat Staffel — $13.95

CAPTAIN SATAN
☐ #1: The Mask of the Damned — $13.95
☐ #2: Parole for the Dead — $13.95
☐ *NEW:* #3: The Dead Man Express — $13.95

DUSTY AYRES AND HIS BATTLE BIRDS
☐ #1: Black Lightning! — $13.95
☐ #2: Crimson Doom — $13.95
☐ #3: The Purple Tornado — $13.95
☐ #4: The Screaming Eye — $13.95
☐ #5: The Green Thunderbolt — $13.95
☐ #6: The Red Destroyer — $13.95
☐ #7: The White Death — $13.95
☐ #8: The Black Avenger — $13.95
☐ #9: The Silver Typhoon — $13.95
☐ #10: The Troposphere F-S — $13.95
☐ #11: The Blue Cyclone — $13.95
☐ #12: The Tesla Raiders — $13.95

DR. YEN SIN
☐ #1: Mystery of the Dragon's Shadow — $12.95
☐ #2: Mystery of the Golden Skull — $12.95
☐ #3: Mystery of the Singing Mummies — $12.95

MAVERICKS
☐ #1: Five Against the Law — $12.95
☐ #2: Mesquite Manhunters — $12.95
☐ #3: Bait for the Lobo Pack — $12.95
☐ #4: Doc Grimson's Outlaw Posse — $12.95
☐ #5: Charlie Parr's Gunsmoke Cure — $12.95